ATTACK

P A WILSON

Ebook ISBN: 978-1-990509-05-6
Paperback ISBN: 978-1-990509-04-9
Audio book ISBN:978-1-990509-06-3

FREE EBOOK

Claim your copy of Running the Game when you use the QR code below to sign up for my newsletter and cheer on Pen as she vies for a commission in the military.

Kalin stared at the screens in the observation lounge. The view didn't change; it wouldn't be any different until they approached the planetary system containing their new home. Or that's what he hoped. If the view did show something other than stars and black, it would mean the enemy might be able to see them.

And he wouldn't take bets on their ability to survive.

His counselor told him that sitting here was unhealthy, but he had nothing else to do. If the captain gave him an assignment, then he wouldn't need to hide here. As much as it made him feel like a coward, Kalin couldn't deny that's what he was doing. Hiding.

His friends were busy. Even if they weren't, he needed to find independence. Walking the corridors was a nightmare. The best he could expect was for no one to notice him. But few did. When people nodded in acknowledgment or offered a smile, he couldn't believe they were sincere. Most just looked away. He saw the pain of the losses his own people had inflicted. There were times when he wished he had been on the ship when the enemy attacked. Being dead might be better than this half existence.

Kalin, report to the captain's briefing room.

He rose to face the corridors. Disobedience was not an option, no matter how much he wanted to stay.

KALIN ENTERED A FUNCTIONAL SPACE; his anxiety dropped with the more familiar surroundings. No room on his old ship, *The Righteous Storm*, held personal items. The room itself held a table that could seat twenty people, monitors on the wall, currently blank, a dark gray carpet, and a white board for planning. Kalin felt at home in the room.

So, not a private meeting. Roger Whitnal, the civilian leader for the ship, was there too. He'd been instrumental in Pen's last assignment. Was that the way the future would be? The civilians working with the military. Kalin had no idea how to assess the situation. His old ship had no civilians.

"Kalin, take a seat," the captain said. "We have an offer for you."

No assignment? Kalin took the seat and waited. Whatever the captain asked him to do, he would agree.

"You do have a choice," Whitnal said. "We think this would be the best use of your skills, but if it doesn't work out, we can keep looking."

"What is this assignment?" They could call it an offer, but Kalin would not think of it that way.

"Now that we are on the way to the planet, we need two things," the captain said. "A way to defeat the enemy if it comes to a fight, and a way to recognize them early to avoid a fight."

"Why do we need a new identification process? We have the scan the analysts set up," Kalin said.

"Think it through, Kalin," the captain said.

The scan for elements worked, Kalin thought. He'd been part of the team who figured it out. "Because the only thing we know for sure is that it detects their presence. What if those elements are present before one of their ships arrives?"

"Yes," the captain said. "I am glad to see we were right in our estimation of your analytical abilities. We want you to lead the team tasked with these two goals."

"What kind of skills will the team have?" It might be difficult to free up the expertise needed.

"We gave considerable thought to the composition of the team," Whitnal said. "We are asking you to be the co-leader."

"I will do as you order, captain," Kalin said.

"I heard a 'but' there." The captain said the words without censure, but Kalin heard it anyway.

"People will not accept any solution I design," Kalin said. "They distrust me at best."

"That is something for us to deal with," Whitnal said. "Don't worry about what people think. Is this something you can do?"

With enough time, Kalin thought. The assignment would be something to fill his days. "Who else will be on the team?"

"You'll co-lead with Lieutenant Brianne Stonehouse," the captain said. "You are a lieutenant now. Your team is made up of specialists from a few ships."

Kalin looked at Whitnal. The man seemed to accept this was a military operation. Did he forget the problems from a few days ago, when four civilian girls felt so excluded that they almost destroyed the entire fleet?

"Are there any civilians on the team?"

Whitnal smiled. "No. The skills lie in the military for the security of the fleet. If you require specific skills and the best is a civilian, we will make them available."

"We need to know today, Kalin," the captain said. "The work is critical."

"You ask for my decision," he said, "yet when I tell you I'm not the right person for the job, you ignore me."

The captain looked away, then turned back. "I did hear your objection. I think you need some perspective about what people think of you. Do you have any other objections? Questions?"

Kalin looked at his hands. Thinking became easier when he wasn't looking at the captain, a position he'd been trained into obeying without question. Having objections in his old life was dangerous. Even a suggestion could be seen as dissent. But that was his old life. He needed to start living this new life, otherwise he would never fit in.

"Does anyone on the team know you are assigning me?"

Whitnal leaned forward. "Are you concerned they won't work for you?"

"Yes. And so should you be. You may think I am overestimating the hatred I face, but I killed people. Relatives of people on this ship."

The captain looked at Whitnal before saying, "I told both Lieutenant Stonehouse and the members of the team that we are asking you to co-lead. No one objected."

"Perhaps if we put a civilian in as a co-leader," Whitnal said, "it will alleviate the problem of perception."

"The military are trained in warfare," the captain said. "Your scientists are fully qualified in their fields, but this is about war in the end, and that's our job."

There was some conflict between them, but they kept it hidden. Kalin couldn't fight his conditioning any longer.

Trying to think of ways to change their minds required practice.

"I will accept the assignment," he said. "When do I start?"

"The others are already setting up in the strategy and planning room." The captain stood and motioned for Kalin to lead them out. "Let's go introduce everyone."

2

Brianne waited until the captain and Whitnal left the room, and she was alone with Kalin. The killer. The enemy. She couldn't ask the questions she really wanted answered. Why were the civilians involved in a military operation? Protecting the ship and fighting, if and when an attack came, was the military's job. They might be going for a planet to colonize, but today they were in space. Whitnal couldn't understand the hard decisions that would need to be made.

More important than civilians getting in the way, was the man who stood staring at the notes on the wall. Why did they appoint Kalin to the team? Why as a co-leader? He couldn't be trusted. He'd only been on the ship a few weeks and before that, he was slaughtering the people they now asked him to protect.

"This is a good place to start," Kalin said, like she needed his approval. "But it's just one option."

"We agreed this morning, before you got here, the ship should deal with this threat in space. We know what to do here. An unknown environment like a planet might be more trouble than help."

He turned away from the notes and sat three chairs away from her. "We may not get the chance to decide where we engage."

She weighed her answer. She enjoyed a good debate, but he needed to understand she was the person in charge. Brianne didn't know what the captain told Kalin, but it didn't make sense a stranger would head an important assignment. There were things the captain couldn't say aloud, but she knew how to read his true meaning. Kalin was here for some kind of image thing.

"If we make it happen, we can. I don't think something important like this should be left to chance."

Kalin looked around the room. "When is the team coming back? We need to keep talking about all the ideas."

"When they've finished the jobs I gave them." She sat up straighter. "You and I need to talk about what's going to happen."

He frowned and looked at the wall again. "We have an assignment. We find a way to identify the enemy early, we find a way to fight them, in space and on planet."

"Nothing is that clear cut," she said. "The captain wants us to find the enemy and destroy them."

He kept looking at the board, but now he tapped his fingers on the table. Brianne waited for his next stupid comment. This was going to take longer than she thought.

"Why do you think that?" he finally asked. "The captain gave specific orders. He repeated them only moments ago. Nothing he said pointed to aggressively hunting an enemy that could destroy our ships the way it did mine."

Our ships?

"He didn't have to say the words," Brianne said. "If you

knew him well enough, you'd understand. Sometimes the real job can't be spelled out. We are to keep the new home safe from any threats. The way to do that is to take them out in space before they learn our destination. The colony won't survive if it has to live under the threat of attack forever."

"I'm used to following orders I'm given," Kalin said. "Trying to figure out if there's a hidden meaning can get you punished."

"Yeah, your old life was pretty oppressive," Brianne said. *Be careful, he will run to the captain if you tell him too much.* "It didn't work out so well for them."

He flinched. Brianne looked away to hide her smile at his pain. Maybe he'd back off now.

"We should follow orders," he said. "If your ideas of what the captain wants are right, he'll pick your option anyway."

Why didn't he get it? "We don't need to waste time and energy on different plans. I'm right."

"And Mr. Whitnal? You think his agenda is the same?"

Now he was looking right at her. Brianne felt doubt rise. Kalin wasn't going to be pushed around. That made him a problem — and a scapegoat. She could find a way to blame him when things went wrong.

"It doesn't matter what he thinks; the captain is in charge."

Kalin stopped tapping the table and looked down, thinking.

Brianne kept quiet. She'd misjudged him, so it was time to listen. She would still get her way; she just needed a change in tactics.

"I may have been on this ship for a short time, but I have worked with Mr. Whitnal. It is not a smart move to dismiss him. I think he very much agrees with the captain right now.

When we approach the planet, he might change, but at this moment, he's better served working with the military."

Brianne held her first reaction back. Perhaps letting Kalin learn the truth was a better approach. He didn't need to know she'd be working behind his back and getting her plan approved.

"How long do you think it will take to come up with some ideas on the other options?" She would give him a couple of days to dig his hole.

"You got the team this far in a couple of hours," he said, pointing to the notes. "It shouldn't take long to catch up with other ideas, but you've been working with the team. I haven't met them yet."

She smiled, this time not bothering to hide it. "I expect them back after lunch. I've got something to do until then." She walked out, not waiting from him to comment or offer to help.

3

K alin left the planning room after making a few personal notes on the work done so far. He needed thinking time, and food. He made his way to the front of the dining hall and ordered a sandwich and a tea.

He wondered if he should take the tray back to the room when he noticed Pen waving at him from a large table in the corner. His mood lifted at the thought of spending time with her. He took his lunch over and sat.

"Hey, I heard you have a new assignment," she said. Her pad beeped and she glanced at it before flipping it to privacy mode.

Pen was only a few days into her own role. Being the 'voice of the fleet' seemed to agree with her. The frustration and confusion that drove her before were gone from her face and her voice.

"How much do you know?" The captain hadn't said it was classified, and Pen should be aware of the details, but Brianne's words echoed in his head, causing him to doubt his interpretation.

"You and a team are trying to find a solution to the new threat," she said. "Find ways to identify their ship early and then how to kill them without losing any of our ships or people."

Everyone had their own slightly different interpretation. Kalin thought back to his orders before, when the people around him were the adversary. Nothing was open for discussion. The orders were always clear: *go to this place, do this thing.*

"You probably shouldn't talk about it in public," Jo said as he joined them. "Kalin doesn't need to be inundated with every idea anyone has about his job." He placed his tray on the table and sat beside Pen. "It's not a secret, but I guess it makes sense to keep the work to the experts."

"I think it's important to look at a wide range of options," Kalin said. "My co-leader is intent on following one strategy. Perhaps a few more points of view would be good."

Pen peeked inside his sandwich and made a face. "Believe me, you won't get anything done if you let the whole fleet in on it. But I'll keep an eye out on my messages for anything that might help."

"Who is your co-leader?" Jo asked. "Pen, are you hungry?"

She shook her head and tasted a spoonful of his soup.

The little acts of intimacy felt like there was no room for Kalin in Pen's life. She would plan a future with Jo, and Kalin wanted her to be happy.

Kalin told them about his meeting with Brianne. "I'm hoping the team isn't all of the same opinion."

Jo looked around. No one was close, but he leaned in when he spoke. "I don't know her, but I've dealt with people like her. Be careful. She'll take all the credit and dump all the blame on you."

"I don't care about credit," Kalin said. "We need to get this right."

"And it's leadership's job to choose the option," Jo said. "Her way is likely to put us in more danger because you'll be sent back to the beginning if the captain wants more."

"Any tips on how to bring her onside," Kalin asked, and after a moment's thought, "or get the team to do the right work regardless?"

Jo scraped the last spoonful of soup up and then crumpled his napkin in the bowl. "I don't know how I can help. I'm heading out with the scouts soon. We're patrolling the edges of the ship's sensors. I'd appreciate you finding a solution, so I don't get to be the first one killed."

"Have you met your team?" Pen asked.

"After lunch."

"Don't push them to take sides. Be calm and tell them what you want. Don't get into a fight with this Brianne, and find a way to separate the people who are aligned with her from your team without making it look like you are splitting the group."

Kalin laughed and wished for simpler times. "So, do exactly what I am saying not to do?"

Jo received orders to report to the scout bay and then Kalin and Pen were alone.

"You must have some ideas," Kalin said. "It is sort of what you do every day, right?"

"I always tell the truth," she said. "Of course, the truth comes with different aspects. Keep in mind the end goal. If you don't care about credit, show her that she can have it. And one more suggestion."

A cleaning mech approached the table. Kalin pushed the empty plate to the edge and added his own dishes. "Is it to go to the captain? No. I must show him I can deal with my own problems."

"You think I wouldn't suggest you ask for help from the captain? Is your memory gone? I just got released from medical from the last time I ignored that choice. He will give you advice. But, yes, you need to show him what you can do."

Kalin had no idea what else she could be suggesting. Too many things in his life changed. This ability to talk freely around superiors. The existence of civilians who weren't slaves. Every time he thought he'd gained some ground, it slipped away.

"Okay, what are you suggesting?"

She sat back in her chair and looked at him, catching and holding his gaze. Whatever it was, she expected him to reject it and maybe get angry. Then it clicked. "Oh, Asher. You think he can help me."

"Yes. This is his thing, working around people's set ideas. Getting the right result no matter what gets in the way."

And doing it with torture, drugs, or something worse... kindness. "I don't trust him."

She leaned in. "He saved my life, and I still don't trust him. Look. As far as I can see, he's a regular guy until he's given an assignment. And, frankly, I've never seen him do all the things we've heard about."

And he knew the ship inside out. "I don't want her handled," Kalin said. "I'll try Jo's way first."

"Fine." Pen looked over his shoulder as she spoke. "Crap, I have to go. Did I tell you they gave me an assistant? More like a monitor."

She jumped up and hurried to the door where an ensign was waiting with a pad held out. The man definitely looked put out at having to find Pen.

4

"Oh, group, this is Kalin," Brianne said. "I'll let you all introduce yourselves as we go along."

It was obvious from the way everyone looked up that he'd disturbed a conversation. The team was supposed to be busy for another half hour. Kalin wanted time to talk to Brianne before they arrived. He didn't want an audience while trying to turn her to his way of thinking.

"Sorry I wasn't here to meet you earlier." He looked at Brianne as he said it. "Can we take a moment to catch me up?"

He saw a flash of something defiant in her eyes and tight mouth. Then it disappeared. "We were brainstorming a few ways to dig into the ideas from this morning."

She pointed to the list on the wall. There were circles and names now. They'd been working for more than a few minutes.

"I think the captain is looking for options to choose from," he said. "This seems like one approach." He turned to look at the team sitting around the table. Seven people. Enough at this point, but they would need engineers when the project moved to operational status. When the captain, and probably Whitnal, chose their best plan. "Does anyone have alternatives?"

He didn't look at Brianne, but the anger was like a wall pushing at his back.

One hand went up. "Lee Mukherjee, sir." She stood and nodded at everyone like it was a presentation. She was, like most of the people on the ship, dark skinned, brown eyed, and about a hundred sixty centimeters tall. Her eyes flicked to Brianne and back to him. She straightened and said, "I think we need to at least anticipate that the enemy will find us before we find them."

Kalin nodded, and before he could speak, Brianne said, "We can't plan for something not in our control, Mukherjee."

Lee deflated, but three more hands went up.

"I'm not sure that's the case," he said. If he continued to work this way, Brianne would snipe at every suggestion and people would stop speaking up. "Why don't we try something? Why don't I work with the four people who have other ideas, and you can work your option with the rest. Then we will create something to talk through. Say by the end of shift?"

Brianne stared at him. Lee stood and grabbed a handful of markers and a pad of paper to attach to the opposite wall. Brianne watched every move.

If she objects, I will push.

"Good luck with it," Brianne said.

"Before we start, "Kalin said, "we should probably introduce ourselves."

Lee put the pens on the table and pointed to herself. "You know my name. I have a solid background in chemistry and physics."

"Mordecai Chan," a man who looked only a few days out of the training program said. "Long range scanning, communications, data analysis, and encryption."

"Elissa Owusu. Physics and biology." She didn't look up from her hands held in her lap, her dark hair falling in ropes to cover her face.

Kalin wondered if it was lack of confidence, or something else.

"Gavin James," the last person said. His skin was so pale Kalin wondered if he was ill, and his red brush-cut clashed with the flush on his cheeks. "Intelligence and code breaking. Military side, of course."

Why is Brianne so happy to let them join my team?

"I suggest we drop any rank propriety," Kalin said. "Just first names and everyone can talk freely. Everyone gets a chance to be heard."

They nodded, and as one, turned to face the blank sheet of paper.

"Where do we start?" Elissa asked. "Anything other than the other team's ideas?"

At least she didn't have a problem speaking up when it came to work.

"We can trust them to do that one," Kalin said. "We'll make notes if there's any crossover. You are the experts; what's the first idea?"

Lee wrote in the middle of the sheet, Long Range Detection. "If we can't find them, we can't do anything."

"If we can't find them, they can't find us," Brianne called. "You should worry about defeating them."

His team looked to Kalin. "Not time to evaluate yet."

"Are there other materials around the destruction site?" Gavin asked. "I mean, are we sure no one held back data when they shared with the public?"

"There is," Kalin said. "A lot of blood mist and body parts, but the data will be there. I'll ask for full access."

"Dead bodies won't tell you anything," Brianne said.

"Keep going," Kalin said. He turned to Brianne. "Can I talk to you outside?"

He watched her mouth move to respond but she thought better of it.

When they were standing in the corridor, Kalin checked to make sure they had privacy. No one loitering, but who knew what security measures were active. "I thought we agreed you would develop your idea, and we would come up with other options. The captain makes the decision, and he won't be satisfied with only one recommendation."

He hadn't meant to lecture, but his frustration with her pushed the words out.

"I was giving feedback," she said, innocence painted all over her face. "I thought that was our agreement. You would come up with ideas and we would critique them."

If this was his old world, aboard *The Righteous Storm*, Brianne would be reprimanded and punished for insolence. Of course, with her attitude she might not have survived to be like this.

Patient and professional.

"At the end," Kalin said. "We need traction, and if you keep giving feedback, we will never work out a plan."

"You don't know how things work," she said. "I'll let you waste time, but you won't get approval for any cowardly idea of running and hiding. Maybe that's what your people did. We need to show these assholes they can't kick us around."

Kalin took a breath as grief mixed in with his frustration now she'd brought up his loss. If he couldn't keep his emotions in control, it wouldn't end well.

"My people were not weak. If this enemy could be killed easily, we would not be faced with this danger."

She glanced back into the room. Kalin kept his gaze on her.

"Fine. Half an hour before shift end," she said. "You've got three hours to convince me."

I don't need to convince you.

Inside, his team had almost filled the first sheet with interconnected ideas.

The day hadn't gone much better, but Kalin counted it as a win because his team didn't desert him, and Brianne didn't destroy all their ideas. Tomorrow, his team would start early and go through the data available to them. The last time he'd looked at it was when the whole fleet worried that the enemy was lurking to attack. Without that fear, maybe it would be easy to find the clue they needed to take the next step to the next clue.

Now, he was going to meet Pen for dinner. Since everyone else he counted as a friend was gone or too busy with their other roles, keeping in touch with Pen was important. And she didn't need to do anything; just being with her helped.

A picnic in the observation room was the break he needed. A few other people stood watching the screens today. The room had filled in the days after the attack, but watching stars and black didn't hold people for long. He picked a table in the far corner so they would have privacy.

"Hey, good call," Pen said. She unloaded their dinner

from the tray onto the small table. Three salads, three bowls of stew, three pieces of cake.

"I thought it was just us," Kalin said, stuffing his disappointment down and grabbing a chair for the mystery guest. "Did Jo receive different orders?"

She concentrated on placing the meals at three settings. "No, he left with the scouts a couple of hours ago."

Kalin didn't know anyone else who might be joining them.

"Asher," Pen said. "Don't get mad. He can help and he won't do anything unless you ask him."

Can I believe that? Kalin figured if the answer was yes, the question wouldn't be in his mind. He looked to the door. Should he leave? There was no sign of Asher yet. "He works for Whitnal."

Pen sat and took the wrapping off her salad. "Yes. He worked for him when he helped me find those girls. And when he rescued me. He never lied to me, and he never betrayed me."

"So how did you put aside your feelings?" Kalin took the chair facing the door. "I know you didn't trust him when you came to rescue those survivors. I saw your face when you thought he was going to torture me. When he offered you the job, you didn't trust him even though he helped save your life. Now you two seem like best friends."

"Fine," she said. "You're right. It took a while for me to drop the suspicion. I guess I still wonder about what he does for his day job. But you saw how he helped. Can't you take something from that?"

Learning by the mistakes of others was familiar to Kalin. The fact that Pen was saying she didn't make a mistake trusting Asher didn't mean he wouldn't turn on them. "I don't want to add another person to the mix that I need to watch out for."

Pen glanced over at the door. "He'll be here in a minute or so. Please, hear him out. He knows how to deal with people. I swear he won't cause you any more problems."

Asher entered the room and looked around. He smiled and waved when he noticed Pen.

"No promises." Kalin decided to listen. He could always walk out.

"I don't have much time," Asher said. "Thanks for the lunch, Pen. What's the problem?"

"This can't go further than us," Kalin said. When Asher nodded, he shared the events of the day. "I need to figure out how to work with her and stop her undermining my team."

Asher pushed the salad aside and dug into the cake, nodding as he chewed like he was analyzing the data.

Probably is.

"Okay, here's what I think is happening. Although, remember, I've only heard your interpretation and that adds a bias." He pushed his empty plate to the middle of the table and started counting out the points on his fingers. "You got clear orders from the captain. You think your job is to come up with a few choices and then act on the one the captain chooses. Brianne interpreted the orders differently and is sniping at your ideas. You are afraid of the consequences if she is successful — or right."

Hearing the experience back so plainly stated helped, but Kalin wasn't ready to put aside his feelings about Asher. "If we don't get it right, we face a battle we can't fight, let alone win."

"Where's Whitnal in this?" Pen asked. "I'm surprised he isn't working with the captain."

"He is, but I report to the captain. This is an all-military team." Kalin wondered if that made sense. Was there an all-civilian team working on the problem?

Asher smiled like he'd read Kalin's mind. "He agreed the civilians don't have the expertise or access to do this alone. And right now, he's on the same side as the captain."

"Might be an issue," Pen said, "but that's not why we're here."

Asher took a forkful of Pen's cake. "This is so good."

"How are you not fat?" she asked.

"Good genes. So, you want advice or actual help?"

Help might cause more problems. "Advice will do."

"Okay. For some reason she is feeling territorial. I don't have any background on her — I could look for it?"

"Just advice."

"You are right that she's putting us in danger, but you'll waste your time trying to convince her. I suggest finding a way for her to feel like she can win, one that keeps her out of your way."

"I don't care who gets the credit," Kalin said. *And I don't plan on wasting time worrying about it.* "What kind of background check would you do?"

"Nothing too intrusive. I can go deeper if I bring Whitnal into it."

"If I need someone with authority, I'll talk to the captain."

"Okay. I can look at her records. Not only the official ones, but the private notes. If she's been transferred for anything like this before, it should help."

"Why would she be on the team, let alone co-leader, if she has this kind of history?" Another weird way this fleet worked. If Brianne is a known troublemaker, she should be reeducated, not given responsibility.

"She could be working to undermine you for some reason," Pen said. "Another attempt at sabotage?"

Asher glanced around before speaking. "There are no indications of another plot. I think we'll start seeing political maneuvering soon, but no one is going to endanger a future they want to control. And there's nothing to sabotage, yet. I'll stay alert for any whispers, but that won't happen until you have a plan."

Kalin agreed to the background check and Asher left.

6

B rianne walked through the planning room door, a tray of snacks in hand. If she couldn't get rid of Kalin, she'd out-nice him.

Everyone in the room stood around Kalin's papers that now lined the walls. Her team was going through a list of ideas, making suggestions. Not pointing out flaws, but actually making good suggestions.

"What's going on?" she asked, trying to keep her voice light. She put the tray on the table and dragged a smile onto her face. "Did you find something useful?"

Kalin stepped away from the teams and joined her at the front of the room. Her team continued to work, as if she hadn't spoken. He'd won before she even started fighting.

"Thanks for the treats," he said. "We've been at it for a while."

Everyone came in early without notifying me? "Did I miss the memo?"

He looked back at the team. "They all just drifted in. I was here early digging through the data, thinking I'd have some quiet time. Then this happened. Good, right?"

Good? He wanted her to be happy he'd stolen her team and would now steal all the credit?

"Castle, Bianchi, and Sousa are my team and should get back to their assigned work," she said. "Like you said, we can't just offer one option."

He didn't react. Didn't he understand what she wanted? It couldn't be possible that he really didn't care about credit. How did he expect to advance? When they landed on a planet, she was going to hold a position with power, and the only way for that to happen was for her to be the one who found the weapon to make them safe. Or, be seen as that person.

"You have a few more things for us to look at," Kalin said, pointing to her own three sheets of notes. "We thought we'd go through ours first, try not to waste time with bad ideas."

"And my ideas are bad?" It was getting impossible to keep her temper in check. He'd stolen her team, he thought her solution was useless, and he'd be the one who solved the problem.

"I didn't say that. Look, no idea is bad until we put up a lot of ideas. Some of them need to be weeded out, so we can spend our time on solutions that have a chance of working."

"How long are you going to keep them working?" She nodded to the group chatting across the room. "We don't have a lot of time."

"I've asked them to pick three that seem promising. They are discussing the final one now. We'll come look at yours soon."

And her team would be all excited about what his found. "I need my people back now so we can prepare for your input."

He called her team away, and they took their time leaving the discussion.

"I think we've picked," Ensign Sousa said, looking back over her shoulder. "I have some thoughts on our solution, too."

Castle and Bianchi followed her, put another sheet of paper on the wall, and started making notes.

"How long do you need?" Kalin asked. "We'll work until you are ready for us to check out your idea."

Could she improve more than one on the wall? Could her team refine one of Kalin's ideas?

"An hour. I need to focus them again."

Kalin rejoined his team and kept working. Brianne stared at the pages on her side of the room. *One idea is not enough.*

"What did they think was good?" she asked.

Ensign Sousa turned to face Brianne; the other two seemed happy for her to speak. She glanced over at the other team and then back at Brianne. What was she hiding?

"They focused on identification," she said. "I guess it makes sense that we need to find the enemy before we can take them out."

So, little crossover between our approach and theirs.

"I think they are close," Ensign Castle added without turning his head. "Are they going to present first?"

Not until I can get some credit.

"You keep working," she said. "Those new ideas are great. Figure out how we present to the captain today."

She left her team and crossed over to join Kalin. One idea or addition was all she needed. One thing she could point to so the captain would know Kalin didn't do all the work.

Kalin moved aside to let her read their ideas. There were twenty or more of them scratched on the paper. "How did they get this far so quickly?"

"I told them to rest, but apparently they hung out last night and pulled ideas from the data we gathered."

Now they were throwing challenges at the ideas. No one seemed to care who came up with it. "How many do you want to present?"

"Three," Kalin said. "But we'll keep everything documented in case anyone asks for more. What do you think? Your team got their say, you should too."

She wasn't going to argue him out of giving her a chance to undermine him.

"Adding power to the current identification process seems the easiest, but how do you know it will work?"

"We'll test it. There are some pieces of debris that weren't part of my ship, so we're assuming it's part of the enemy. *The Righteous Storm* would have taken advantage of even the slimmest chance to fight back. I expect we'll find some evidence of them in there too."

And they lost.

"If you analyze some of that debris, you might find some additional indicators."

"Already started," Kalin said. "What about the idea of leapfrogging the scouts to extend our range?"

"Are there enough scouts? And are we going to sacrifice them? I mean, unless we find a better way to locate the enemy, we'll only know there's a problem if a scout goes dark. And that might be anything, from comm failure to death."

"They're working on refining that one. No one wants to recommend it, but we needed options."

"What about leapfrogging visuals?" Brianne pointed to the clustered notes. "Your team thought about it as a verbal communication. What if the scouts sent back visuals? They could escape fast after a sighting, or they can send drones to the farthest points, and we don't risk a pilot."

That is enough to get me recognized.

"We could do the whole thing with drones," Kalin said. "A much better option. Especially if we don't have to see the enemy. That's what the other ideas are about. A way to identify without getting close enough to be seen."

"You think maybe there is some kind of communication between enemy ships?"

Kalin wrote the idea on the wall. "If we could go back and record the events leading up to the attack, it would help."

Brianne smiled. *Another way for me to take the credit.*

7

K alin looked at the listed ideas on Brianne's team wall. She still wasn't considering any other options, and most of the new ideas she'd crossed out. This couldn't end with a single recommendation.

"It looks like you've left the identification part to us," he said.

"Finding them is only part of the goal," Brianne said. "You made enough options for the captain."

He reread what she'd spent her time on. "I see mainly variations on 'blow them up.'"

The captain walked in, followed by Whitnal. Everyone stood to attention and waited.

"We hear you've got something to present." The captain waved his arm to include both lists of action plans.

Brianne stepped forward and saluted. "Yes. Kalin has done some good work. We can show you the ideas on location tactics and a few early ideas on defense."

Why didn't she just call it what it was: attack. There was no defense against the aftermath of this enemy's actions. He agreed that they needed to destroy anything they found. Her ideas were on point; her behavior wasn't.

"We're ready," Whitnal said. "Kalin?"

He walked to the papers and circled the names the team decided were the top three. "We can get a test ready fast on any of them."

He waited for the captain to read the sheets and ask his questions.

"Looks to me like they are interlinked," Whitnal said. "Leapfrogging the scouts somehow and finding key indicators that will give us advanced warning of the presence of the enemy."

He's as good a tactician as anyone in the military.

"They aren't mutually exclusive," Kalin said. "We need to know three things before we can rely on any choice: how far the leapfrog can take us from the ship, how much lag time, as even a few seconds could be vital, and what we need to design and build the object we test."

"I like the two ideas," the captain said. "A second analysis of the foreign artifacts could be done today. But we could also just take one of those items beyond our range and try to detect it. And the components we already know are alien, of course."

Brianne smiled and nodded like she was agreeing with everything the captain said. "I thought that the idea of using drones and video would save a few lives."

"I'm sure everyone gave input," the captain said.

She glanced at Kalin, then pulled her attention back to the captain. "Yes. A team effort. Do you have a preference?"

Whitnal was standing in front of the wall, leaning in as if he couldn't quite focus on the writing. "Why not all of them? We can't waste time doing one test after another. If the test works, I don't see how it matters if it's the material, or the physical damage, or something we haven't identified. Nothing here is big enough to affect the scout's range for transmitting or return. Most of this is data. Some of the physical pieces are limited, but surely there's enough to create multiple sensors."

Brianne stared at the wall, her mouth tight. Then she blinked and relaxed. "There is a need to know what worked," she said. "Sorry, I don't mean to contradict, but I just..."

Why doesn't she simply say it?

"Lieutenant, no one is going to take offense. This will only be solved if everyone can argue a point. What do you need to say?" Whitnal seem not to notice or care that Brianne was angry.

"I know we're focusing on detection. Kalin's team did a great job coming up with these ideas to test, but we need to destroy this threat. That means we need all the information we can gather. Who knows if the clue to winning is in there with the successful detection? I think we should test everything separately."

Kalin waited for orders. Creating three tests was no more difficult than creating one.

"Is your contribution only about killing them off?" Whitnal asked.

"Someone needs to be working on that," Brianne answered. Kalin detected a snap in her voice. She did not like to be challenged, but she found challenge in the most reasonable question.

"I apologize," Whitnal said. "Poor choice of words. I mean, did the two teams focus on different detection ideas, or did you split into detection and elimination?"

"Getting a head start on the end goal seemed like a good idea," she said.

The captain beckoned Whitnal from the wall. "It is, but now we have some deeper digging. I think it would be wise to set aside the ideas on winning until we know how to find them. I believe detection will lead to identifying weakness."

At a casual glance, Brianne would seem calm and professional. Kalin noticed the stiffness of her stance and her tight control on her reaction.

"I agree," she said. "I recommend we take as little time as possible preparing for the test. We don't want the enemy finding us. They know how to destroy our fleet."

The captain nodded and then glanced at Kalin. He hadn't missed any underlying tension. He knew how to avoid engaging and making things worse. Kalin smiled in gratitude. Brianne would be ten times more difficult to deal with if she felt dismissed in front of people she wanted to impress.

"I'll leave you to your task," the captain said. "Roger and I will find you a few experts to help out."

After the two men left, Brianne kicked the chair in front of her. "Well, let's get to it. Clearly the captain wants this done first."

Kalin ignored the words and put a clean sheet of paper on the wall. "What do we need? Only a couple of hours left until end of shift, and we're working in a tight window."

Brianne was left standing alone at her side of the room as the team members gathered to toss out new ideas for testing.

8

W hat have we forgotten? Kalin stared at the screen, waiting for something to change. One day, not even quite that, to devise and initiate a test. The scout ship with the various materials aboard had been gone for two hours; tracker turned off, comms down. They had no idea where in space the scout waited. Just like the enemy.

The scout would turn on the tracker and comms in another hour. The remaining scouts were patrolling and scanning for the material. If they found it, the fleet was one step closer to safety. If not, they'd start again. The rejected options were too vague for him to feel happy about implementing them, but that was not something to worry about now.

"Even if they do find the items," Brianne said, "it won't help if we have to point the scanner right at the enemy ship. Space is too big."

They sat in the planning room with the whole team and no one else. Kalin wanted them free to react, no matter what the result. Having the captain with them would put restraints on them, make them think before celebrating or grieving.

"I'm trying to keep those kinds of thoughts inside," he said to Brianne. "If this is a success, then we can tweak things all we need to. I hang on to that thought."

She shook her head and kept looking at the screen. He waited for her to tell him he should think of the worse outcomes, but she didn't speak.

Fifteen minutes since the scan commenced. He wanted to get up and pace. To talk, to do something to pass the time. Staring at the screen wasn't going to make a difference. They would hear the results before seeing them. Any contact would set an alarm in this room and one other. Yet, he couldn't take his attention away from the blank screen. He couldn't stop holding his breath every few seconds. It was like going into battle. Time slowed when you desperately needed everything to speed up.

He stretched his legs under the table and started to think about how to get everyone ready to dive back into the work. Maybe come up with a new test, one that didn't need to be rushed.

A shrill whistle jolted him. It slid up and down a scale and ended in a trill.

The screen stuttered and then settled on the target scout ship. The pilot wouldn't know they'd found him until he turned on his comms again, but everyone else knew the test was a success.

The door opened and the captain followed Whitnal into the room. "Well done," he said into the yells of excitement.

It took only seconds for everyone to come to attention.

"At ease," the captain said, waving his hand to the chairs. "We'll have all the data in an hour. I asked the analysts to look first, but to do so quickly."

"We need some refinements," Kalin said.

"Yes, but you also need to celebrate. Take the hour to grab some food and enjoy the moment. We'll be elbows deep in the next steps after that."

SHE DIDN'T WANT the test to fail. Not really, but why did Kalin get all the credit?

Brianne watched as the team strolled through the door after taking hours to celebrate. They all agreed to put in an hour after regular shift to organize for the next day. Everyone loved Kalin right now. She wanted the team focused back on her before the end of that time.

"Now we should work on the weapon," she said. "I know there are tweaks after the test, but we can't be left with the only result being that we know the enemy is around."

Her share of the team drifted to her side of the room.

"It's not just tweaks," Ensign Owusu said, looking Brianne in the eyes instead of keeping her gaze firmly on the desk. "We can't simply abandon the work to a couple of people."

Where did she find that backbone? And why didn't Kalin speak for his team?

"As far as I can see, there are deployment questions, and maybe range. A few engineers can work those out. The captain offered help."

The door opened and Pen Tromarin entered like she owned the place.

"Hi, just looking for some quotes for the announcement," she said. "Don't let me interrupt the great work."

"It was a team success," Kalin said. "You should put in everyone's comments."

Was this a way to take credit for being the nice guy? Or

was something going on between them? Pen stood close to Kalin; he kept glancing at her.

Brianne turned to look at her list of weapon concepts. They wouldn't want her to give a quote for publication.

"I heard the end of the conversation," Pen said. "People will need some reassurance that any tweaks have priority."

"To be honest, there's not much work to be done on the detection part," Kalin said. "Brianne is right; we should pass the next steps to the engineers and focus on what we do with the knowledge."

Brianne turned back to the room. If he was going to give credit, she'd take it and make her official recognition more than a mere casual mention.

"My team came up with the idea of using drones to carry the detection. It won't matter if we lose a few, and the scouts can run back to their ships when something happens. The last thing we need is to lose scouts."

Pen made a note and smiled up at her. "I'm sure the scouts and their families will appreciate that thoughtfulness."

"Time to get a weapon designed," Brianne said. "I made some progress but, as Kalin says, this is a team effort."

"True," Pen said, still looking at her pad. "Lieutenant Stonehouse, right?"

Brianne nodded. "Do you want some details on the weapon ideas?"

Kalin shifted from where he was standing.

Good, he thinks he can get the credit for my ideas. Nice guy, my ass.

"It's enough to say you're focusing on it, I think," Pen said. "Wouldn't want to get people excited about something that might change as you learn things."

There is nothing to learn.

Kalin said something to Owusu and then joined Brianne and Pen. "We'll prepare a report for the engineers. I'll let the captain know we're passing it along to them. If you want quotes, Pen, you should gather them before everyone gets dug into the next steps."

Pen nodded and approached the group of people huddled around the table. The papers from Kalin's group were now spread out, ready to be cleaned up and included in the report. Everyone, even the people who were supposed to be on her team, was contributing.

9

Kalin paused at Pen's door. He took a deep breath, hoping it would give him energy. Brianne's constant fighting was draining. She didn't do anything overt, anything he could point out to stop her, only small comments designed to belittle the work his team did.

Maybe this evening Asher would tell him how to deal with her, or maybe explain how he'd read the situation wrong. The captain put Brianne on the team, and he wanted success, so she must have value.

The door opened and Pen stuck her head out. "Are you going to wait out here all night? The food will get cold."

He smiled. At least he still had people he trusted in his life.

Inside, her quarters were hardly big enough to hold all three of them, let alone the dinner spread on the bed.

Asher leaned against the wall to his left. Pen pointed to the only chair, but Kalin shook his head. Sitting down might tell his body to rest. He needed to be alert.

"Suit yourself," Pen said. "How was today? It didn't seem like you were celebrating that much."

"We were, but..." He reached for one of the sandwiches Pen had wrapped in a napkin.

"Something to wash the food down?" Asher asked, reaching under the desk for a bottle. "Home brew?"

Kalin accepted the beer. He was off duty until tomorrow — unless some great idea woke him up. "Did you find anything out?"

Asher finished his drink before answering. "She's moved around a lot. I know a few of her coworkers. I won't tell you who. They aren't doing anything wrong, but it might look that way."

Pen threw a balled-up napkin at Asher. "Just spill. We don't care where the information comes from. And you'd probably lie anyway. What's up with her?"

"What she's doing with you is exactly her pattern. She wants credit for everything and blame for nothing. Somehow, she gets away with it. I can't believe all her commanding officers were fooled, but they think she's a golden girl."

Kalin had an idea how she managed; it was hard to pin down the tactics. But surely one of the officers recognized her tricks. "How many assignments?"

"Five." Asher reached for another bottle. "The first was the longest. I think she was honing her skills. Although that makes her sound Machiavellian, I don't think she started so organized. It looks like she had a few successes and liked the feeling. After that, she got her choice of deployment. I think she was choosing the commanders she could manipulate, not the assignment."

"Do you want me to tell the captain?" Pen asked. "She shouldn't be able to slow you down."

And make her a real enemy?

"There must be a way to keep Brianne and minimize her

opportunity to undermine the team." This was the most important assignment available. If Asher was right, Brianne would never simply leave it alone.

"She wants to be the hero," Pen said.

"I have no interest in being a star. She can take all the credit."

Pen and Asher exchanged a glance.

"Do you have a solution?" Kalin asked. "If you worked this all out before I got here, just tell me."

"It's your idea," Pen said to Asher. "I mean, it sounds good to me, but you should tell him."

Why is he being so coy?

Asher grabbed the waste bin and swept the remains of dinner off the bed. Kalin hadn't even noticed they'd finished every sandwich and cookie.

When the bed was clear, Asher sat. "This isn't only about saving the fleet. Remember my job? I hear a lot of things others think are secret. People are angling for position on the planet. Now that we're so close, everyone realizes how big a change the future will bring and how many opportunities for power they can grab."

"Sounds like mutiny," Kalin said. That was something he would take to the captain. "Is she involved?"

"This isn't mutiny," Pen said, "and the captain knows what's going on. They aren't looking to overthrow the military. They are simply aligning themselves so when the power jobs are handed out, they take them."

"Sounds like it's more of a threat to Whitnal," Kalin said. "Not only him, but all the civilian leaders."

"That's why I'm getting close to the people stirring up the crowds," Asher said. "Not everyone is grousing, but there are a few surprises. And Brianne is behaving too much like them for me to think she doesn't have her eye on a planet-side role."

One more thing for me to try to understand.

"You need to give her a way to take the credit," Pen said. "She won't believe you aren't interested. She can't understand how anyone wouldn't care."

"Not just to win," Kalin said. "She wants me to lose, right?"

Asher nodded.

"I can ask the captain to let me rearrange the teams." It was the only way to give Brianne a clear path to win.

Pen kicked his shin, not hard, but the sting startled him out of his thoughts.

"You don't need to ask," Pen said. "Just talk her into your way of thinking and then tell the captain."

"I can't get used to having so much freedom. Any at all, really."

Asher stood and took a step to the door. "Keep trying, or you'll give Brianne what she needs, and you'll disappear into the background. No one is willing to admit it, but you still have to fight to be seen. I don't mean just figuratively. What she's doing will keep feeding her ego and she'll escalate to achieve what she wants."

"If I handle things right, I can stop her getting worse?" Kalin did not want the responsibility, but no one else was in a position to act.

Asher opened the door and peeked out. "You can make it someone else's problem. Someone who can deal with it," he said as he left.

"What are you going to do?" Pen asked, touching his arm. "I mean, I had no idea about the last bit. Asher might be blowing the problem out of proportion."

Kalin stared at the door. When he came into the room, he thought the problem was a personality clash. That he needed a few skills to make it go away. What Asher predicted about her escalating didn't sound as ridiculous as he expected. "She's gotten worse. He might not be completely right, but he's not stupid."

10

Brianne walked into the planning room ten minutes later than she agreed last night. She did want to sort some things out with Kalin, but she didn't report to him, so he couldn't tell her when to show up.

He looked up from his pad when she slid the door closed with a clunk.

"Good morning," he said, smiling like she hadn't held him up.

How did this guy who was raised to be a killer keep his temper? "Sorry I'm late." Maybe that would provoke him. If she could get him to react, he would look like the bad guy.

"Not a problem. I had some ideas about how we can move forward." He projected something on the wall. "We need to be efficient and that means no more duplication."

"So, you'll agree to focus on my solution?" She refused to look at the projection.

He pointed to the wall. "Your idea is promising. I think we need to split the teams differently. If we can agree, then the captain and Whitnal should be okay with it."

With no choice other than to look at his proposal,

Brianne pulled out a chair and scanned the new team structure. *He's talking about taking one of mine.* "You're sidelining me," she said, feeling the flush of heat in her face betray the calm tone she struggled to keep. "You are stripping my team and giving me nothing to work on. I won't let you do that."

"Actually, it's the opposite," Kalin said. "Give me a second to explain. I'm pretty sure you'll be happy."

She crossed her arms and slouched back in the chair. There was no way he could twist this into something she'd want.

He walked to the wall and pointed at the diagram with two teams and a list of tasks. "Yes, I'll need one more person," he said. "You can choose who I take. Everyone has skills. I'll work with one team to come up with the ideas and potential development plans for weapons. We should start with the basic decision from the captain on where we plan to meet the enemy."

"Space. It makes no sense to bring them to our new home."

"Yes, space is one option. The other is to be ready if we need to fight them when we are on the planet. Maybe we don't need to risk hunting them. Maybe they are gone and we're safe."

"Maybes will get us killed."

"When the captain, and I guess the civilian leaders, make the choice, we come up with weapons. It's a creative process, and we can't afford to second guess every idea. That's where your team comes in."

"What, shooting down your ideas? What if we have something to add?"

He paused. Good, she was getting to him. Pushing him to fight back would work well if the team came in at the middle when Kalin looked like he was causing the problems.

"There are things that need to be done every day, and we can't stop a creative session to do the admin. I suggest you take that on too, but it's not just shooting down the ideas. We'll start with everyone brainstorming. Then my team goes ahead and develops the concepts and your team critiques."

He's going to let me write reports and poke holes in his work? And take all the credit in the report? He's naive. So easy to manipulate.

"You think the captain will agree?" She looked closer at the way he'd assigned the teams. His choice from her people was Jim Bianchi. "You can have Wilma Castle. He has some final procedures for his gender reassignment but should be available enough to contribute. I'll call the captain to ask him to approve it."

"We have an appointment in a couple of hours. I want to talk to the team first." He adjusted the names on the wall and left the presentation stuck up there.

No argument about personnel? He is serious about this cooperation.

She turned and pulled down the sheets of paper from her wall, placing them on the table for Kalin to take. "If my team is supposed to do the admin, we should be the ones talking to the captain and making appointments."

He looked down at the desk but not before she saw him smile. So, he thought handing her the admin was a victory. He didn't have a clue that she now owned every piece of communication coming out of the team. And she who holds the pen holds the power.

"I'll get some refreshments sent in," Kalin said. "Probably a good idea after the celebrations."

He left her to the room. His pad was still unlocked. She took the large sheets of paper and folded them in four to make them easier to handle. She told herself it would be a bad idea to snoop. He trusted her right now, and that's what she wanted.

"Morning."

The word pulled her back to the room. Castle and Chan walked over to check out the presentation. "You've been busy."

As much as she wanted to say 'yes' and let them think it was her idea, Brianne didn't want to get caught out when Kalin told the group. It was clearly his idea, and there would be better credit to be taken later. And if this all went pear-shaped, she didn't want the blame.

11

Kalin let Brianne enter the captain's briefing room ahead of him. Anything that would help her feel important. She'd shown no sign of undercutting his new structure when they explained it to the team. She smiled now like she was happy. He wouldn't be lulled. She was still the same woman who spent all day sniping.

"At ease," the captain said. He was sitting at the head of the table with Whitnal to his right.

Kalin relaxed his stance from attention, but Brianne grabbed a chair and sat. No one commented, so he did the same. He expected her to start talking but she looked at him.

"I know you need a decision," Whitnal said. "But if we can delay for a few moments, we also have news."

Kalin nodded and looked to the captain. The captain nodded at Whitnal. What the hell was going on? One of them should be in charge of the meeting.

"The detection device is operational. The scouts were all fitted as soon as the engineers were satisfied with their tweaks."

"Good news, sir," Brianne said. "That allows us to concentrate on a weapon."

"Yes, lieutenant," the captain said. "Is there something new we can add to the official announcement?"

Brianne looked at him again, so Kalin explained the recommendations for the new structure. "I don't know if that's worthy of fleet-wide communications."

Whitnal chuckled. "It's not that slow a news day. How do you feel about this structure, Lieutenant Stonehouse?"

Kalin braced for her to betray him. This was the best place for her to achieve what she wanted. Credit, and a reputation for being the only person who identified critical problems.

"It's efficient," she said, "and worth a try. We have time to reorganize if it doesn't work. But I think it will."

The captain tapped his fingers on the table, a short beat that Kalin thought he should recognize but didn't.

"The most important thing is for us to be able to defend ourselves if the enemy finds us. To do that before we arrive at the planet, we need more than a weapon."

"Is that still the approach?" Brianne asked. "To lead the enemy to our home?"

"Not lead them there," Whitnal said. "This decision is final, yes. We are going to the planet, and we are hoping the enemy doesn't find us."

Kalin watched Brianne's lips move, ready to argue. But after a glance at the captain, she decided not to speak.

"Sir, what did you mean not just a weapon?" Kalin wasn't going to leave anything up to interpretation. He didn't want to waste time arguing with Brianne about what that meant.

The captain stood. "We need a strategy, too. There's no point having a weapon if we don't have a plan to use it, or a plan to avoid using it."

In the past, his orders had been straightforward actions. The elders worked out the strategies. "Then we need to focus on a different goal," he said.

Brianne spun her chair to stare at him. "What do you mean? The goal is to kill the enemy so we can be safe."

"Yes. Explain," Whitnal said. "If we change the decisions we made previously and start again, we are lost."

Kalin kept his eyes on the captain as he said, "I misspoke. The goal remains the same, but we need to express it differently. Right now, we are saying that the goal is to find a weapon. So, we focus on weapon design. If we restate the goal as keeping the fleet safe from this unknown enemy, then weapons are only part of the solution. We broaden our view to include defensive measures, misdirection and anti-detection, among other things."

The captain nodded and shifted his gaze to Brianne. Kalin wondered if he was completely aware of her personality issues.

"It's a new way of looking at it," Brianne said. "We're going to use up time to pull people back from the current solutions."

"We don't have time to get it wrong," Whitnal said. "But I'm sure your team is capable, and if you need more people, I can suggest a few who are excellent at misdirection."

"It would help if someone with expertise took a look at what we come up with," Kalin said. "I think Brianne will agree that adding people right now when we are refocusing is probably not productive."

I'm not ready to deal with Asher on a daily basis.

The captain checked his wrist. "I need to go to another meeting. Is there anything else?"

Kalin gave Brianne the opportunity to speak, but she was frowning at her pad as she read her scribbled notes.

"I think that's all," he said.

The captain thanked them and Whitnal rose to leave.

A klaxon sounded and the wall screen lit up.

"They've found us," Whitnal said.

Kalin read the data on the screen. "No. We've found them. A drone. This result is a long way from us, and from any scout. This is good. We know they can't sneak up on us, and the drone self-destructed after sending the results."

"We need this sent to the planning room," Brianne said. "What about the rest of the fleet? This is going to cause panic."

"It's just here," the captain said. "The scouts, the analysts, and engineers received the news, but that's it."

"We'll get back to work," Brianne said. She tapped her pad and closed it. "Permission to use stims if necessary, sir."

"Agreed, but be careful, lieutenant. Overuse will cause errors in logic. We need people focused, not hyped."

"Aye, sir. I'll manage the distribution and keep records. In fact, perhaps a medic could monitor what I'm doing."

"I'll send you a link to someone I trust," the captain said. "You report every dose. Come on, Roger, we have some engineers and analysts to calm down and some scouts to debrief."

"You did that well," Kalin said when they were alone. "I would never have thought of stims. I guess until we needed them."

"I do know what I'm doing." She turned to the door and left him standing alone.

12

"There's something more," Kalin said after confirming the new structure to the team.

"It's good and bad," Brianne added into the pause.

He waited for her to continue with the information, but she stepped back. This was stupid. The project came before any of her games.

"The alert system worked," he said.

The rustling of paper and shifting of pads that he'd hardly noticed before stopped and everyone froze.

"Yes, the test," Wilma said. "We know that."

"Not the test," Brianne said. "Lieutenant Castle, we don't have time to repeat information. We expect you to listen."

Wilma cleared his throat. "That means we found them? We're not ready."

Brianne sighed. "Yes, we've found the enemy, which means we need to focus tighter on the goal. No, they don't appear to have found us, which means we have time. Maybe not much, but some."

She knows how to do this, if only I could trust her not to twist the communication.

"The captain also reminded us that the goal isn't simply to kill the enemy," he said. "We need to survive. We are still racing for the planet. We need strategies as well as weapons."

"Get to work," Brianne said. "Bianchi, Sousa, with me. We need to set up some kind of organization to this mess."

Kalin joined his team. The ideas flowed better when they wrote on the flip chart paper tacked to the wall. Once a plan was approved he'd use the screen, but for now, ideas were important.

Elissa Owusu sorted through the pile of used papers. "Here it is," she said. "We should put the original weapon idea up."

"The weapon isn't the first priority," Lee Mukherjee said. "Strategy. How will we avoid a fight? How will we fight in space? How will we fight on the planet?"

Kalin heard Brianne's influence in Lee's tone. "How we do this is more important. All ideas are valid until we find a gap. Everyone here is capable of discarding truly unhelpful ideas."

Lee blushed. "Didn't mean that we shouldn't look at the weapon, sorry."

"I know," Gavin James said, "but we can't waste time thinking about how we say things either."

"Then we agree not to take offense and not to be purposely offensive," Wilma said. "Is everyone okay with that? Or am I overstepping, sir?"

Kalin grunted a laugh. "Let's put rank aside. I'm Kalin here. And you've already shown you're better at this than me."

"Then first names unless higher ranks are present,"

Mordecai said. "I'll put the weapon stuff near the door, to give us room to work." He didn't move.

"Is there something you want to say, Mordecai?" Kalin asked. "We need to air things to get the whole picture."

Mordecai flashed a glance at Brianne's team. "Just a thought. Are we sure these are the aliens who destroyed your ship?"

"They were present," Kalin said. "There's no doubt about that. We built the detection tool from data at the debris site. You think they came later? To see what was going on?"

"No. I guess I'm not so comfortable that we know enough about whatever or whoever is out here to be sure."

"We can't risk it," Lee said. "They didn't give Kalin's ship a chance to do anything but die."

My ship wouldn't have taken a chance to do anything other than fight.

"Okay," Mordecai said. "It was just a thought. I'm behind our plans one hundred percent."

Lee put a title on the single blank sheet. "Maybe we'll come up with something. Let's start with strategies for avoiding a fight."

Ideas flew at her, leaving her no time to add her own. Kalin took the marker. "Keep going. When we run out of ideas, we'll narrow down and then move on."

AN HOUR LATER, the entire wall was covered in paper with comments circled or scored through.

"Are we ready for critique?"

"Let's tidy it up a bit," Gavin said. "It needs to be more like what will go to the captain for decision."

"Does anyone mind working through lunch?" Kalin asked.

"I'm not stopping now that we're so close," Lee said.

Kalin placed an order on his pad for lunch to be delivered. He watched as three clean sheets of paper went up, one for each strategy chosen.

"Bianchi, Sousa, keep working on the database," Brianne said. "We'll need to create a presentation, and I don't want to lose any information."

She stepped to Kalin's side and waited for the last points to go on the wall. "Which one do you think we should take to the captain?"

Kalin paused for a breath. He thought this was settled, but she wouldn't let it go. Now he couldn't be sure anything they'd agreed on was final. "All three. Are you asking which one I think has the best chance?"

She huffed. "Yes, I am aware we don't get to tell him. You've made that clear."

No one showed any signs of hearing her comments. Kalin didn't believe it was more than an act. Even if only to learn what more senior officers were thinking, ensigns would be listening. If there were sides, no one wanted to pick the losing one.

"They all come with risk," he said. "You can point all that out in a minute. I don't think there is a best choice. Or not yet. Whatever gets picked will be developed and become the best choice."

"Ready," Elissa said. "Shall I take notes?"

"Sure, Ensign Owusu," Brianne said, stepping closer to the wall. "I'll have Bianchi clean it up."

Brianne read the three sheets of ideas. "Let's start with this one," she said after a few minutes. "Status quo. It relies on luck, and that's dangerous."

"It's no worse than the others in that," Kalin said, "but it is the current strategy; we can't ignore it."

"It's a stupid strategy," Brianne said.

Everyone found something interesting to stare at as the words left her lips.

"It is what the leadership of the fleet decided," he said. "I am not going to tell the captain he chose stupidly. I will give him choices now that we are not reacting to the initial shock of being a target."

"Oh. I thought you said no idea was wrong. I was just expressing my thoughts," she said, dripping in fake innocence.

"Is there something concrete you can point out to show it's not worth placing on the list?" He wasn't going to argue the point. The team didn't need to witness their disagreement over style.

"The plan is reactive," she said. "You know I want to go on the hunt."

He didn't comment.

"This second one," she said, moving to stand beside the middle sheet of paper, "isn't much different. We just go faster to the planet. Some of the ships are at capacity now. And what then? We get there and hope for the best?"

"We don't know the enemy's capability to fight on a planet. You haven't been on a planet, right?" he asked. Unable to resist reminding her the only living people who'd been in a real alien atmosphere and felt natural gravity were the rescue team, the survivors, and him. "It's completely different. The gravity well might be enough to dissipate the power of their weaponry. They may not be able to survive outside their ships."

"Still a lot of luck needed," Brianne said, "but I guess we still need to create a weapon. You weren't thinking of ignoring the threat, right? We'd still be prepared to fight?"

Kalin nodded. He wanted this stage over with. They

were done with developing strategies and needed a decision. Despite what she seemed to think, it wasn't fear of fighting the enemy keeping him from agreeing with her attack plan. He knew enough about battle to not be eager for it. Fighting meant death, and she had no idea how that affected anyone who survived.

"This last one is another hide and hope plan," she said. "Why didn't you include my idea of hunting the enemy?"

So that was part of the problem. Her idea wasn't there.

"We don't have enough information about them to attack," Kalin said. "No matter what weapon we develop, we won't be sure if it works until we use it. And if we fail, we all die."

13

Brianne needed just one or two more points to place her fingerprints truly over these solutions. She gave up on trying to convince Kalin to only present one option. It just meant finding a bit of each solution to be able to take credit for no matter which the captain chose.

"What happens if we end up fighting them on the planet?" she asked, stalling for time because there was no way he'd be able to give an answer.

"We need a distraction. Maybe try to convince them we are gone. That way they might not keep looking. When we land, our first priority is to find places to hide."

"You should put that up," she said. "You don't want to leave out important points."

The door to the room opened and she turned away from Kalin to see Roger Whitnal entering.

"Can I have a minute of your time?" he asked. "I don't want to delay you, but we need some details for the communication."

"I guess that's my job," she said, stepping away from Kalin. "You can go back to fleshing out the solutions."

"This needs both of you," Whitnal said. "I promise it won't be more than a few minutes."

This man could be leading the colony. Not a good idea to antagonize him.

"Of course," Brianne said. "What can we do for you?"

"I thought it might be a good idea to give the team some accolades," he said. "I don't know if any key people were involved, but a bit of credit can help motivate someone."

"I would prefer we simply praise the team," Kalin said. "There really isn't one person who contributed more than any other."

Fool

"Well, I was working with the team for a day before Kalin joined us," she said. "I suggested leapfrogging the signal, for instance."

"I'll make a note," Whitnal said. "I have the names of the team members, perhaps we can arrange a quick interview with some of them. Later today, of course. That doesn't need to be part of the initial message."

"Can I ask why you are the one asking?" Kalin asked. "Isn't it Pen's job, or one of her unit?"

Whitnal smiled and nodded. "I confess to a bit of curiosity. I asked Pen to let me drop by. What's on the agenda now?"

"We'll report to you and the captain in a bit," Kalin said.

"It's some strategies to win a battle with the enemy," Brianne said. "I'm sure the captain wouldn't mind us talking to you about it."

"No, I'm happy to wait. We don't want your boss thinking I'm sneaking behind his back."

He didn't come for that. There's an agenda here.

"If you had some guidance for us," Brianne said, "it would certainly help us narrow down choices."

"I see three groups on the wall. I'm sure that will be sufficient." Whitnal didn't try to move close enough to read the papers, and it wouldn't help anyway; they were in a scrawling shorthand.

"Then we should get back to work," Kalin said. "Brianne will reach out for a meeting as soon as we are ready."

"Good." Whitnal closed his pad.

"One thing," Brianne said, before he could head for the door. "Anything new from the scouts? Are they all back?"

"Not yet. You'll receive the information as soon as we have it."

"Maybe we can interview the scout who got the identification?" Kalin asked.

Why can't he shut up?

"Don't wait around for that," Whitnal said. "Will you need us to be available tonight?"

"Tomorrow morning," Brianne said. "I know we're under pressure, but I don't want to rush and make a mistake. I need to review and assess Kalin's recommendations."

"Until tomorrow." Whitnal nodded his head and then left them.

"We could be ready in a couple of hours," Kalin said. "It's only lunch time."

"And there are a ton of questions to answer before my team starts compiling the information."

He kept his eyes on her while he thought about her words. The man was so transparent. He was annoyed about letting her use time to pick his work apart. To find a way to make her choice the clear winner.

"Fine," he finally said. "We should start answering your questions."

"No. Go figure out how much of that planet-side plan is missing and fill in the blanks."

Was he going to say she wasn't the boss? Had she pushed him far enough to make him lose that infuriating calm?

"You are right. There are gaps. Will you join us or are you busy with the admin?"

She bit the inside of her cheek to stop the smile of triumph. "Call me back when you have something for me to assess."

14

The presentation meeting for their strategies was first thing in the morning shift. Brianne gathered her thoughts before walking up to the room containing all the information needed to answer any question that might come up. She'd spent hours creating the presentation, slanting it in her favor. As long as the captain didn't look too closely at the details on the wall, she would win this one. Winning meant recognition for having the right strategy and for thinking ahead with her plans for the weapon.

"Don't stand on ceremony, lieutenant," the captain's voice broke through her daydream. "We're all anxious to hear the results of your work."

"Yes, sir." She held the door for him. Whitnal strode up behind the captain and followed him through. Like she was the doorman. They'd be sorry for that when they realized she'd saved the fleet.

The team members sat together at one side of the table. Kalin was sitting and looking over something on his pad.

Perhaps her draft presentation. She sent it a few minutes ago to avoid him giving input.

"I think we are all ready," the captain said. "Let's start."

"We have strategies worked out for three options," Kalin said. "As we narrow down the choice, we will add more detail. If you can choose the first steps, we can move forward."

"Which is your preference?" Whitnal asked.

Why did he need to be here? Brianne didn't understand the civilian mind. Would the same methods work to bend him to her choice? Would he look impartially at the military options, or was he too eager to get to the planet, where he would be in power?

"We all have different opinions," Kalin said with a smile. "I'm glad it isn't our job to choose. I think it's better if we keep our preference to ourselves until the end."

The captain smiled and Brianne hated Kalin for it. She kept her face and voice calm. "We have three approaches. Perhaps you can explain, and then we can answer questions."

He nodded for her to move to the next page of information. "In order to get into the details of contingencies and backup plans, we need to look at all options."

"This looks like the decision we've already made," Whitnal said. "Didn't we agree to continue to move toward the planet and develop a weapon, hoping never to use it?"

"When we worked on the contingencies and backup ideas," Brianne said, "we realized there were more risks and benefits, and two new options came to light as we went through the process."

"Yes, moving at our current pace to the planet isn't as safe as we thought," Kalin said. "We can find a way to hide from the enemy, maybe, as we continue moving through the galaxy until we feel the threat is gone, but we can also race for the planet we've identified."

"And what are the contingencies?" Whitnal asked.

Why wasn't the captain taking part? Had he decided to go with Kalin's preference? Had Kalin told him what they'd discussed? *I should have sent a copy to the captain making my choice clear.*

"That's where I come in," Brianne said. "When Kalin's team started working through the different ways to keep us safe, it was clear that the tactics we developed could be used on any of these options, but none that applied to more than one choice. Since we are determined not to hunt and kill the enemy, we need to ensure we do everything to avoid encountering them."

"It may be too late," the captain said, finally entering the conversation. "We can't be completely sure that they didn't detect the drone."

"I agree." She flicked the presentation forward. "If we continue as we are, which is the approved approach, we are at the most risk."

"What did the team come up with as secondary tactics?" Whitnal asked.

I might as well have slept last night rather than taking stims. They aren't going to let me guide the meeting.

"As you can see, we focused on the two new options," she said, finding it hard not to say 'I focused.' It was too obvious. "Hiding and traveling until we lose the enemy, or there is no evidence that we are still a target, comes with the main risk that we will never feel safe, and that we won't be able to find a planet when we do."

"And eventually we need a home," Whitnal said. "The ships won't last forever, and not all are as well maintained as this one. What is the benefit?"

She had to find a way to make this a good choice. Kalin was going to recommend racing for the planet. This was her only other choice.

"The galaxy is full of planets," she said. "The scouts can be deployed to check for habitable ones. If we keep moving, we're hard to find. Kalin's people were stationary, we know that at least."

Whitnal nodded. "And it comes with the benefit of not being a race. People will begin to panic when we speed up, and not all the ships can."

He might have his uses after all.

"And the backup plans?" the captain asked.

"We will have a weapon. We will have a list of planets we can use as a home when we are finished." She looked at Kalin, willing him to stay silent.

"And the other choice? If we run for the planet?"

Kalin spoke before she could answer. "The weapon is still good for design and build; the specs will include discharge through an atmosphere as well as in space. We may outrun the enemy, but we will have plans to fool it into thinking the fleet was destroyed in an accident, and we will be defending our home. And the enemy may not arrive or be able to attack us if we are not in space."

It all came out in a rush, leaving no doubt what he recommended. Brianne noticed that his team was leaning toward him in agreement, looking eager.

"I've heard enough. You, Roger? Have you decided which you prefer?" the captain asked.

"Yes, I think we should race to the planet as Kalin suggests. It seems to give us the best chance of survival."

"I agree. Good work, team. I expect details on the idea that we've been destroyed in an accident — draft plans at least. I admit I find it intriguing." He led Whitnal out of the room.

How does Kalin do it so effortlessly? Her work in slanting the presentation was a waste of time and energy. Supporting that stupid run and hide plan made her look like an idiot. She got the decision she wanted, but not the credit.

15

K alin was grateful for Pen's call asking him to meet her in the observation room. Since this morning he'd longed for a way to get out of Brianne's sight. She didn't say anything. Every time he looked at her, she was bent over the stacks of paper generated by the brainstorming or absorbed in her pad. He couldn't rid himself of the thought that she was willing him to fail.

"I'll be back in a bit," he said to the team, not sure his words got through their focus on some specs he couldn't understand. He glanced at Brianne. She looked up from her pad and frowned then nodded.

He felt no guilt about leaving them; he was no use right now. The details on weaponry and analysis of misdirection were beyond him. Far from helping, he was getting in the way. Lunch would be a good way to refresh his calm. And he didn't get enough time with Pen. Although, he was sure they wouldn't be alone.

As he opened the door, his pad signaled a message. He

heard Brianne's do the same. He turned and walked toward his meeting while he read.

Eyes only.

He saw Brianne's name in the list of recipients along with Roger Whitnal and Pen.

Assessment of the fleet's capacity to enact the plan.

The eleven ships in the fleet were listed.

Nine had green status. One orange and one red. *Tomorrow's Promise.*

Action initiated: evacuate Tomorrow's Promise within twenty-four hours and abandon.

He stopped walking. This made everything real. Where was the population of the ship going? No, the important question was, how can we make use of this opportunity to defend the fleet?

He hit reply all and started typing. Before he finished, a new message popped up. An answer to his question. Brianne. Same thought, but she hadn't included everyone in the thread.

He cleared his message and read the reply.

Ship will be available to your team until the distance becomes more than a half-day flight.

At least they had the same question, and he didn't face an argument. Using the abandoned vessel to test some of their assumptions was more than a gift; it could make the difference.

He typed a new reply, sending it to everyone.

Thank you.

Then he sent a private message to Brianne.

Good catch. I'll be back within the hour. Can you start the team on fleshing this out without confirming we're abandoning a ship?

Yes. Need the captain to approve discussion with team. I'll take care of that.

Nothing showed the conflict between them.

THE OBSERVATION ROOM was empty except for Pen and Asher. Fewer people came every day, and that worked well for Kalin. Having a place to meet that didn't take them to the unused areas of the ship or force them to squeeze into Pen's tiny quarters was a luxury. Asher joining them was not so much of a surprise.

Pen looked up and smiled, then stood and gave him a hug. "I wasn't sure you'd still come."

"I'm just in the way there, but I need to go back soon."

Asher handed him a sandwich. "Before Brianne screws everything up?"

"It looks like she's with us now, but this morning something was wrong." He told them his impressions of the meeting.

"You need to be stronger," Asher said. "She's up to something, and maybe she'll back off if you are more confident."

Was his desire not to fight with her a weakness?

"You think she's going to sabotage us?" Pen asked. "Don't be paranoid. That would be suicide."

Kalin chewed while he listened to them talk it out.

"Nothing that big," Asher said, "but little things get out of control. I'm worried her sniping will cause something she didn't intend. And no one will notice soon enough to stop her."

"You could be right," Kalin said. "This morning, it felt like she had a plan and we derailed her. Or the captain did. I know it's getting in my way, trying to deal with her while we look for a way to survive."

"Just be aware of your blind side," Asher said. "Your old life was about following orders, but people are still people. You must have had some team leaders you didn't like."

'Like' didn't matter before. You obeyed orders. But now, looking back? There were a few.

"Think about how you managed them. It will give you perspective."

"I didn't manage anyone."

Pen looked at Asher and chuckled. "You didn't recognize you were, but I guarantee you did."

"I'll take your word for it," he said.

"The latest news is good," Pen said. "Don't worry, Asher knows and we won't be overheard."

"The captain will announce soon," Asher said. "He wants Pen on *Tomorrow's Promise* first. Handling the evacuation."

Now his last friend was leaving, and he was alone.

"I'm on a shuttle in an hour," she said. "I'll be back."

"We've got permission to test some plans on the ship. The team is learning about it now. Brianne is asking for permission to tell them but if not, we can set the test up as a theoretical until we receive the all-clear."

"I received the answer," Pen said. "Did you discuss that question with her first?"

"We had the same idea," Kalin said. "She types faster."

"And she didn't include everyone." Pen's pad lit up. She glanced down. "My shuttle is leaving early. I have to go."

"I wish I could see you off," Kalin said, "but I can't risk leaving Brianne in charge any longer."

Pen tossed her garbage into a bin and headed out the door with a wave.

"I'm still here for you," Asher said. "Not everyone is gone."

Everyone I trust and care for. "I need to do this on my own," Kalin said.

"No. You need help, and Pen is going to be tied up with her duties. You don't trust me, and that's okay; most people don't. But I am on your side in this."

So not always on his side. "Being here is giving Brianne too much time."

"Good first step."

Kalin's pad buzzed. "Looks like we can share with the team."

16

"Kalin, good timing," Elissa Owusu called as he entered.

Kalin glanced at the wall screen as he acknowledged her. A ship icon was exploding and contracting. Brianne was watching the action and making notes.

I should walk away more often. "You have a plan?"

"When we heard *Tomorrow's Promise* was available, we picked the decoy destruction to test."

"I wasn't even gone an hour and you got this done?" He pointed at the wall. Now the ship stopped filling the screen and he saw the list of tests and the requirements.

"It was the only one we couldn't test any other way," Brianne said. "It's good. I'm about ready to critique."

His team settled next to the screen, alert and ready to answer whatever she came up with. Jim and Andor, normally sitting with Brianne, were not in the room.

"Do you want to hear the details first?" Elissa asked.

"I'll catch up. When you are ready, Brianne."

He caught the glare before she took control. Was it because she didn't like him telling her to start? Or because she hated him using her first name? According to Pen and Asher he needed to appear strong, so he let the questions go.

"If we need this to be a real test, we have to work quickly. We'll be out of range fast if we speed up." Brianne looked at Elissa. "How long before you're ready?"

"As soon as the last person is off ship," she said. "We don't need to stage much. We can trigger an explosion easily. The things left aboard will help to make the test look real to anyone who comes by."

Their favorite plan for a decoy was to take one or more ships out of range of the planet and fake an accident. If the enemy came across the debris, they would think the entire fleet was gone.

"We should leave a shuttle and a couple of scout ships," Kalin said. "There must be some beyond repair, given the state of the ship."

"And make sure some personal items are left," Wilma said. He pointed to a list of requirements. "The debris needs to be representative."

Something else was missing from the list, but Kalin let them talk through what they'd identified. Bringing up the missing material had the potential to stop the discussion in its tracks.

"You need to figure out your end results," Brianne said. "No point in blowing up a ship if we don't know what to look for in the debris."

She is good at this. None of her questions carried a judgment, or a subtle dig.

"We based it on what we found in the other debris field," Lee said.

She tapped the screen, and a list of the materials from

The Righteous Storm popped up. The bodies listed as organic material. Did he feel better that the list didn't say people?

"How will we be sure if the test worked afterward?" Brianne asked. "This is a game until you have concrete results."

The team members looked at each other, hoping that someone would volunteer the information. They hadn't agreed on this point. *Too soon to point out the missing component.*

"We should listen to all the options," Kalin said. "How many are there?"

Lee slid a new sheet on the screen. "We were getting to this point when you came back."

Three points stared back at him from the screen: Does it matter? Leave an observer? Leave a drone and leapfrog response?

"What do you mean, does it matter?" Brianne's scorn was back in her voice, and her mouth seemed to want to twist into a sneer.

Elissa stood. "It does, obviously. We mean, are we testing that the enemy will fall for our ruse or are we trying to see if we can do this and be reasonably sure, if the enemy encounters the remnants, that they will be fooled."

"Are you unsure we are capable?" Kalin asked.

"No. I mean, yes, we can blow up a ship," Wilma said. "Are we capable of creating the scene, rather than just destroying a ship? If we aren't, isn't it better to learn it now so we have time to work on the plan? We can't be sure the enemy will ever find the resulting debris. Here, or when we arrive at our new home."

"We can't leave an observer," Brianne said. "Their presence would defeat the whole purpose."

"And the drone," Kalin said. "No guarantee it wouldn't be followed. Or simply stop working."

"You need to do more work on that," Brianne said. "We can't take a plan to the captain as questions."

"I think you need to frame the idea better," Kalin said. "That's your piece, right? The first point changes to the value of testing our capability, the rest is just risk versus reward. In this case, I think we can sell the captain on the first."

Her lips tightened.

I've done it again. Told her what to do like she reports to me.

"I'm sure you know the best way to do it," he added, hoping the words were enough to appease her. Keeping her happy didn't take much, and he didn't care if she thought it made him look week.

"Within the hour," Brianne said. "We do need to get aboard and see what we're working with."

"There's one important requirement not on the list," he said. "I believe it was called organic matter on the debris list from the last attack."

The room went quiet. No one forgot; they simply didn't want to deal with the reality.

"And where do we find that?" Brianne asked. "Are you proposing we ask for volunteers? Maybe use the sick, or hold a lottery?"

"Have you had a break yet?" Kalin asked the team members, ignoring Brianne's question.

Lee shook her head in response.

"It's going to get busier when we receive approval, so I suggest you grab a bite now," he said

"But there are things we need to work out." Elissa pointed to the screen.

"Yes, you can do that over lunch. I suggest the observation room for privacy. We'll see you back in thirty."

Brianne didn't say anything. He waited until they were alone.

"Where are Jim and Andor?"

"Why don't you answer my question about the bodies?"

"I don't want them walking in on the discussion."

"I sent them for lunch. We'll be busier, too, making this mess into something for the captain to sign off."

"You could tell they were uncomfortable with the idea of adding bodies to the debris."

"Yes, but you didn't seem to be." She pushed her pad away from her and glared at him.

"I am, but there are alternatives beyond what you proposed."

She didn't speak.

"Brianne, is this going to turn into a problem? I sent the team away so we could be open. Did you really think I was proposing to kill people for this?"

"I don't know what you were raised to think. It certainly was not to value life."

There it was. No one in the fleet would ever accept him without a full coating of fear he'd revert to what they thought of as only a killer. "I was taught to value every life. On *The Righteous Storm*, they taught us you instigated the slaughter. Everything you think of me, we believed was true about you."

"So? You still think we need to sacrifice people for this test." She flung a hand at the screen. "It is only a test."

Every instinct screamed at him to shut her down. To get her off the team. To have her held away from the populace so she couldn't do harm. Her emotions pushed her to ignore logic. But every time he acted on his instincts, he reinforced those fears.

He held back the hurt and anger. "Do you not keep your dead?" If anything, his words made her reaction worse, not better.

"They will be shot into a sun," she said, her voice calm, eyes blazing.

"Would they not believe it an honor to serve the fleet in this way?"

Brianne looked away from him. Her hands, flat on the table, released their tension. Minutes passed and her body slowly relaxed. When she looked at him again, her gaze was cold. He couldn't put aside the thought that she'd found a way to make it her idea, and if the plan failed, she would make him the monster.

17

————

Brianne forced her body to relax. She'd gone too far and now Kalin could report her. No other project was important enough for her plans. This one let her be the hero and connect with the right people on the civilian side. This one allowed her the opportunity to find a place high up in the planetary power when they landed. Maybe she shouldn't have kept the stims when everyone refused them. She vowed to wait longer between doses.

"When they were alive, would they not be honored to serve the fleet in this way?" He'd asked.

His question wasn't an attack, no matter what it felt like. He really didn't understand. *Maybe it's not too late to turn this in my favor.*

"I suppose, but there is ceremony. Ways for the survivors to say goodbye. This will be secret. We can't include anyone because they will delay us with arguing." Her hands were curling into fists again. She took a moment, pretending to think, but in reality, she was forcing the tension out. "I loved people in those freezers; relatives, friends."

Kalin sat back. Again, she'd handed him information he could use to weaken her.

"And they are watching. God has them. The bodies are empty." He pointed to his chest. "This is just a vessel."

He believed in God? Hard to integrate with the killing he did. "It doesn't feel like that to those of us who loved them."

She hated the sentimental words, but even more hated the feeling coming over her. When had she become so soft?

"I know that," he said. "As the leaders, it's our job to make difficult facts easier on people. Our team members probably have lost people and are waiting for us to approach a sun. How long since that last happened?"

"It's my job to critique your ideas," she said, more comfortable with the anger than the sorrow. "If you don't like it, we can switch places."

"To critique, yes, but you are shutting down ideas. You criticize, not critique. Will you tell me how long since the ship came close to a sun?"

She considered avoiding the question, but he would just ask the captain, and doing so would reveal they weren't working together. "This ship, fifty years. I don't know about the rest of the fleet."

"We have enough organic material for the test and the real action."

He was cold. He didn't believe the bodies had been people. "Why do you call them that? They were people, not plants."

"On the list of debris from when *The Righteous Storm* was destroyed, that's the expression they used."

"Even so, it would be better not to use that expression."

"You think I like my family and friends being referred to in such a clinical way? Do you honestly think calling the bodies anything else will make this situation better?"

I don't want to make it better.

He looked at the time. "We need to finish this soon."

"What do you want me to do? I think this is wrong, but I'm alone."

"No one is happy to do this. Do you see any other ideas?"

"We can't afford to use any of our food stock or harvests to create the appearance of people," she said. "We need the captain and Whitnal to sign off. And this test needs to come from our dead. If we do use them, we must keep it a secret; we can't ask other ships to contribute."

He smiled, and she knew she'd lost.

"A good point. We forgot *Tomorrow's Promise* will have a supply of organic material. No one will evacuate the dead, right?"

"We still need approval," she said. How did he do that? Just when she thought the game was over, he found a way to give her credit for something she just tossed out. "It would be better. And people would think everything was normal if we didn't move bodies."

He nodded. "If our plan works, we will not be sending bodies to suns anyway. We would be burying or burning them on the planet. Would it not be better to save the colony than be buried or burned?"

"I'll talk to the captain," she said, happy to do it now that the plan sounded like an honor rather than a violation.

AN HOUR LATER, Brianne stood beside Kalin in the captain's briefing room. She'd presented the plan and now waited for his decision.

"We'll need to handle this carefully," he said. "Your plan is solid, but using the dead will be a hard message to hear for their relatives."

"There is no other way to fake that component of the wreckage," Brianne said.

"I agree, lieutenant."

Kalin hadn't spoken during the discussion. She wanted that silence to continue. "Do we have the go ahead?"

"Prepare, but keep the details under wraps for now. I need to test out the response."

Brianne started to say that once underway, they couldn't back out, but the captain held up a hand.

"I understand. Tomorrow morning we'll reconvene."

18

Kalin stood at ease the next morning in the captain's briefing room. Another update meeting, another draw on their precious time.

"We've encountered resistance," the captain said. "Not everyone is willingly evacuating. We need to speed up the process."

"It's not only *Tomorrow's Promise*," Asher said. He'd been brought in by Whitnal, but no one mentioned his role. "Other ships are showing signs that they won't just follow orders. We need to stop the unrest before it gets bigger."

"To be expected," Whitnal said. "They worry that we will abandon their ship next."

Kalin listened, not quite understanding why he and Brianne were in attendance. Yes, they needed to know that there may be a delay, but this wasn't a good use of their time. Some materials they needed for the test were waiting for transport. It was important that the charges dispersed the debris correctly. They needed to plant the various items around the ship while people were still aboard.

"Military personnel are required," Whitnal said. "A few

of my civilian security team members are there, but a uniform can give a sense of urgency and order to the evacuation. The new quarters will be ready in a few hours, so they can move in and get settled."

The unused portion of the ship was more than large enough to hold the evacuees, if what he'd seen during Pen's rescue was any indication. Kalin glanced at Brianne; no indication she was going to ask anything. "How long before this becomes a problem?"

"How long before your test isn't worthwhile?" the captain asked. "I would like everyone aboard and settled a while before we blow the ship."

Their plan didn't take into account any settling in time for the new civilians. He'd assumed the ship would be emptied as fast as possible and then the test would start. Any time taken away now would cut into the three days of data gathering before the fleet moved too far away. And they did need to increase speed as soon as possible. Every hour sitting here was an hour for the enemy to surprise them, and an hour longer before they put down on the planet.

"We need to see if the explosion works as expected," Brianne answered. "If we set drones to record and collect data, we don't need to hang around. But if we can watch and send a scout party to the site, we'll receive higher quality information."

"We accelerate in twelve hours," the captain said. "No later, preferably sooner."

"Then we need to empty *Tomorrow's Promise* in less than four," Kalin said. "Do we need to worry right now about this protesting business?"

"Not urgently," Asher said, "but it's only going to get worse."

"We should subdue the evacuees," Brianne said. "If they

are unconscious, they will be easy to transport. Once they are aboard *Dark Prospect*, it will be too late to resist."

Everyone in the room looked at her. Kalin saw the sense of her suggestion, as anything was better than leaving people aboard to be destroyed. In his old life, when a ship started to fail, no one gave a thought to rescue. But the people he now called his, the fleet, they would riot.

"That's too drastic," the captain said. "We'll go with the military presence and send your team now. As soon as the last shuttle leaves, you can commence."

"And if some people refuse to leave?" Kalin asked. "Should we tell them what is going to happen?"

"The evacuation is not your task," the captain said.

Brianne looked at Kalin and shook her head a little. Was she going to let that pass? They may not be in charge of clearing the ship, but the progress definitely affected them.

"The timeline is critical, sir," Brianne said. "If we miss the opportunity to do this test, we'll be blind when the situation arises."

"If the situation arises," Asher said.

"No, Asher," Whitnal said. "They have to work under the assumption that the situation will occur, not that it might. Do you have a suggestion, lieutenant?"

Kalin waited. He knew better than to suggest leaving people aboard, which was the only other option. Perhaps if he only faced the captain, he could phrase it as a question about how far away the line was on their actions. But not here, not in front of civilians. The military thought more like his old life. Civilians would not consider such a plan.

"They are endangering the fleet," Brianne said. "We've given them more than enough time to gather their belongings. They have no goodbyes to make because they are not leaving people, only a ship."

"Yes," Asher said, "but people tie themselves to a home, and it's not as easy for some to leave."

"By giving them a choice, we are lying," Brianne said. "The other ships in the fleet need to understand that if we determine they need to move, there is no choice."

"What are you suggesting, lieutenant?" the captain asked in a quiet voice.

Brianne didn't catch the warning in his tone. Kalin held his breath, hoping for something that would work.

"If people are determined not to join us here where it's safe, they should be allowed to stay on the ship. The fleet will pull away and we are done."

No one flinched or argued.

"And your test?" the captain asked. "You would lose the opportunity."

Brianne sat straighter and looked at the captain as if no one else was in the room. "If you ordered us to do so."

"No, we can't," Kalin said. "We can't abandon people and we can't miss the test."

The captain held up a hand to keep the others from speaking.

"We will not do anything of the sort," he said. "Everyone on *Tomorrow's Promise* will be transported. Every action to do that will consider the effect on the remaining ships if we have to sacrifice another. Thank you for being the Devil's Advocate, Lieutenant Stonehouse. We now know where our boundaries lie. And it is this side of atrocity."

Was she deliberately provoking to find the limits? She was very lucky they had an understanding captain.

"Return to your plans. You will be ready for your shuttle in three hours." The captain turned to Whitnal, dismissing Kalin and Brianne to their duties.

19

———

Kalin stood in the shuttle bay watching the supplies pass into the cargo hold. Explosives, monitoring drones, and a few bodies because *Tomorrow's Promise* passed a sun close enough to cremate theirs only ten years ago. Those containers were now marked as packing material. No one would give them a second look.

Kalin had taken down the names and family details of the people inside before they were crated. He'd do the same on the empty ship. These people would be honored at some point. Even if he had to personally reach out to every survivor.

Brianne had the leadership of the team for the short while he would be gone. They were working on her weapon design. He hoped that would keep her satisfied.

"Ready?" Asher asked, coming from inside the shuttle.

"I don't know what that means," Kalin said. "Yes, we are as prepared as we can be. Can anyone be ready for what we are about to do? In secret?"

"No. It's uncharted territory for us. I think the idea of destroying a ship is as close to sacrilege as we can get."

For a society run by people who aren't priests, and without an official religion, they use a lot of Christian phrases.

"We'll be quick. Is everyone out?"

Asher nodded. "Yes. The last shuttle is set to leave in an hour. We'll be aboard before that."

"You're coming?" Asher didn't seem the type to dive into the action directly. More a snoop in the shadows kind of person.

"We've been given more time," he said. "I'm going with a team to make sure we don't lose any records. We'll work on data recovery while your team set the charges."

Spying. I should have realized.

"Don't look at me like that," Asher said. "The leaders of *Tomorrow's Promise* know we're going. They agreed. We can't afford to lose any knowledge if we can help it. Every decision from the moment that ship is destroyed will be a no-return option."

"Sorry." Before he could say more, they were interrupted by shouting at the bay entrance.

A crowd of ten or so people shuffled forward and began yelling at the guards who stood in their way.

"Shit," Asher said. "We should board. Are your supplies loaded?"

"What's going on?" Kalin took a step to assist the guards when the crowd kept moving.

Asher grabbed his arm. "They can take care of this; you need to get inside."

"Save our homes..."

"No ship lost!"

"Stop the tyranny."

Kalin turned and looked around. His team was in the shuttle, the last crates loading. "Is this about me?"

Asher pulled him into the shuttle. "No. Well, not specifically. They are protesting the addition of *Tomorrow Promise's* people to our population."

Three more guards joined the defense team, turning the crowd back and clearing the entry, closing the doors and running for the shelter.

"Do they have an alternative?" If anyone in his past had even whispered about such an act, execution would come swiftly and brutally. "Does this happen often?"

Asher instructed the pilot to leave when he was ready. "Get secured," he said. "Our presence is only encouraging them."

"Won't they be detained?" Kalin snapped the restraints closed and checked the others in the personnel area.

"All clear to go," the pilot announced.

The shuttle slid toward the port, now standing open. The alarms in the bay announced their departure.

"I don't understand what happened. How many people think we are doing the wrong thing? What do they suggest we do?"

The team members released their safety belts and checked the equipment. The pilot was an expert; not even a slight bump on leaving *Dark Prospect*.

"The reaction is unusual, but we're doing unusual things," Asher said. "Only a few people are riled up enough to do what we saw, but there are rumbles of discontent."

"If there is a better idea, I'm happy to hear it." Kalin pulled a water bulb from the dispenser.

"If they do, no one is offering to share. Pen will find a way to deal with them. And these people won't burden *Dark*

Prospect mainly because we won't be in space much longer. I guess since we took Loke's people in, it might look like we're doing more than our share. It's hard to imagine people threatening our survival, but remember, they only hear what we give them. If they are inclined not to trust, we get this behavior."

"Aren't we the only ship capable of taking on people?"

The fleet was at war. No battles yet, with luck there would be none, but dissent now put people in danger. He couldn't imagine dissent ever being helpful.

"We're in the best shape," Asher said. "And this won't be the last time we need to cut a ship loose. *Tomorrow's Promise* was just the worst maintained. If we don't hit the planet soon, we'll be squeezing more and more people in."

"Should the captain talk to them? Whitnal?" It felt like no one was acting and by the time he returned there would be riots.

"Let Pen deal with the situation when she gets back," Asher said. "Don't talk to anyone because they'll only twist what you say. We have people infiltrating and it will die down. And we'll be on a planet before everything gets too bad."

That was stupidly optimistic. "I hope you are right."

"It's the sitting and waiting," Asher said. "They can't go anywhere. We don't appear to be doing anything. It will die down when we move."

Kalin sat back and closed his eyes; talking wasn't helping. Asher was too certain in his belief — perhaps he was used to this kind of thing. Kalin couldn't suppress the fear that the fleet would not be destroyed by this new enemy, but by its own faith in people who didn't deserve it.

Maybe Pen would explain. She was on *Tomorrow's Promise*. He'd be talking to her soon; she would understand his alarm. She would convince him that Asher was right, or maybe he'd believe her when she said it would be okay.

20

When they arrived on *Tomorrow's Promise*, and the outer bay doors sealed to contain the atmosphere, Asher headed off with his small team. Kalin knew the pilot would have announced their arrival, but he sent a message to Pen as soon as the bay was clear. His team rolled the equipment onto a transit mech and headed out to plant charges and cluster the bodies in the bridge and a few recreation places, in case the evidence needed to be scattered.

While he waited for Pen to join him, Kalin walked the empty bay. His shuttle stood alone, their pilot waiting to carry everyone back. It looked empty, but more importantly, it felt empty. Kalin had no experience on an abandoned ship. He expected either crowds of people going about their business, or terror and panic as his old unit raced through, destroying every life form in reach. The quiet wasn't peaceful; the bay almost rang with tension. Like something waited for him to drop his guard. Something not human, old and angry and seeking vengeance.

"Hey."

Kalin's heart stopped and then raced. Then his brain caught up: Pen. Lucky he hadn't been holding his weapon. "How did you sneak up on me like that?"

"You were miles away. Creeped out?"

"No, I was heroically battling the various ghouls and wraiths that have taken over the ship."

"I believe you. God. Awful, isn't it?" She waved her arm around the bay. "The bay should be filled with shuttles or scout ships. When we got here to evacuate people, only half of that was usable. Over the years, they jettisoned anything broken after scavenging the parts."

Now they needed to fill the space with some shuttle parts rather than leave the broken ones in place. "They wouldn't have survived long. Even though they resisted, the facts are this ship was done, right?"

"It was still home," Pen said. "It's hard to let home go."

"Do you have time to talk?" He had nothing to do unless his team ran into problems. He was here to give one last check of their work and collect the names of the dead. Well, officially. The real reason was to talk to Pen and to get away from Brianne for a while.

"Everything's done. I'm the only one left on board. I supervised the evacuation. The last shuttle was almost at capacity, and I said I wanted to wait and come back with you."

"We should call for some damaged shuttles to at least partially fill this space."

It was only a test, he knew, but if they were successful, maybe the enemy would be fooled.

"Don't worry, they left enough around," Pen said. "We shoved all the bits in the bay next to this. It was in the way as we sent people on the shuttles. I wanted to make sure no one could hide from us."

"Good."

Now that it was time to ask about Brianne, Kalin found a surprising reluctance to speak. What new advice could Pen give him? And he didn't want to admit his temper frayed to shreds when he thought about the way the woman acted. He didn't want to waste any time with Pen on stupid things.

"So, what do you want to talk about?" Pen looked around as if some chairs had materialized. "Let's sit over there. It will be a couple of hours before we need to do our final checks and then leave."

Over there meant sitting side by side on the floor, leaning against the wall. Kalin went to the shuttle, grabbed two water bulbs, two seat covers, and a pocket full of ration bars.

"Thanks, these will be better than the floor," Pen said, grabbing a seat cover from him. "I'm looking forward to my quarters. Peaceful, and padded. Is this about Brianne?"

Kalin chuckled. Trust Pen to take the initiative and drain the awkwardness out of the subject.

"She suggested we leave the people who didn't want to come. To let them die slowly without support."

Pen drew in a breath. "That's harsh. Did you think she had a point?"

Too complicated for a yes or no answer. "They were endangering everyone. I guess before I was part of your world, I didn't need to worry about what I thought. The elders wouldn't give them a choice. The ones they wanted to save would be saved. The rest would be left to die."

"But you are part of our world," Pen said. She leaned over and bumped his shoulder with hers. "Maybe if you stop comparing, life will be easier."

Was he doing that? Always weighing what the elders would have made him do against what these new people asked him to do? Or was it so simple as thinking of the captain and Roger Whitnal as not the same as the elders?

"I can't just turn off most of my life," he said, "but I can try to let go a little."

"So? What does today's Kalin think?" She kept her eyes on his, not letting him avoid the truth.

"They should be subdued and transferred, and the captains can deal with the fallout later. We don't have time to delay. The enemy could be close. We need to move the fleet."

"But we shouldn't abandon them?"

Isn't that what I said?

"No. Everyone is valuable, and we don't know who will be vital on the planet. I don't understand how people can be so blind to the urgency. We must act now, and debate all we want later."

"They are afraid," Pen said. "It didn't delay us to let them say their piece. Of course, they will be happier on a ship that is actually working properly. The food here was like the bars we took on the planet. Dry, tasteless, but nutritious, and they had to survive on two bars a day."

"Protesters came into the bay when we left," Kalin said. "They know what life is like on a ship that works and have no idea how hard life can get. I still don't understand how they can believe the enemy will pass us by?"

The sound of voices came from the passageway outside. Not close, but he'd soon need to leave to make his inspection.

"I heard about that," Pen said. "It's happening on all the ships. They want a voice in decisions. They think the military is forcing them to shut up and obey."

"They can have a voice when we land," Kalin said. "We'll all be inexperienced, and maybe we'll be safe."

"True. It's my job to start calming them down when we get back. After the test."

"What about you?" Kalin asked. "When we are safe. Will things change?"

"I'll stick with the captain," she said.

The voices were getting closer.

Kalin shifted to look at Pen. "I meant personally. All kinds of new possibilities will be available."

"I'll wait to see what they are," she said. "It would be nice to create a family, but I don't want to think about the future. I'm too busy right now."

"I'd like to be part of your future," he said. Clumsy, but he didn't have much time. He couldn't go through the next days and weeks wondering if she saw him as a friend or if she imagined a future for them.

"I want you with me." She stood and greeted the techs who came through the door to report on their progress before heading off to complete their tasks.

Too late to ask how she wanted him to be in her future. And she was right about being too busy.

21

Brianne looked up from the weapon design specs. Kalin was back. He nodded at her and dropped a sheaf of paper on the desk.

"Test is ready," he said. "A couple of hours and then we head away."

"Yes, I got the message," she said. "The drone will start transmitting right after. We should receive details for two days."

"Any other protests?" Kalin asked.

Something is bothering him.

"You mean like the one that chased you off the shuttle deck?"

He didn't react.

"No," she said. "The evacuees are settling in their quarters. The captain is going to meet with the leaders of the protest. But it doesn't matter. We're on our way."

He nodded. Was he afraid to speak to her? Not possible.

"Did something go wrong on the ship?"

"No. Everything is set. I'm just trying to understand the

reaction. I've been told I spend too much time comparing my old life to this one."

Surprising that he would worry about it and even care to change. "Are you?"

"Look," he said, "you and I hold very different ideas about how things should go. Is it because I'm bringing too much history? I know people still think I'm an enemy."

"We don't agree on how, but we both want to end the threat," she said. "We'll never be friends, but we are on the same side in this."

"What would you have done when the protest started?"

She sat back and thought. Yes, she'd wanted to be the one going to *Tomorrow's Promise*, but her role was to find the errors in the work Kalin did. They made fewer of those as they got further down the line, which was disappointing, but she could make something up if she needed to. The captain sided with Kalin every time. And Kalin didn't fight back in a way she could use to her advantage. Was this the way to win out? To keep his confidence battered? It might not work. All he had to do was talk with his friends and they'd buck him up. But it kept her activities out of sight of the people she needed to impress.

"The same as you," she finally admitted. "It's security's job to deal with unrest. Our job is to save the fleet."

"Will we?"

"Yes," she said. "One way or another. It might not be all the ships, but we'll make it to the planet. We'll use our weapon."

He sat up straighter, nodding to the specs laid out on her pad. "Yes, we will. I'm being morose, and that won't get anything done. Did you make suggestions for the weapon?"

He must have been playing me. No one turns from depressed to practical that fast.

"Some. We need to take into account the density of the planetary atmosphere. If we can gather that data from the original probe, it will help."

"It's worth asking. Everyone is getting ready for the explosion, so we won't receive an answer right away."

Brianne flicked through the specs and pointed again. "The range is too short if we are attacked in space. We can't let the enemy get that close."

He nodded. "There are some things we can do through atmosphere that we can't in space."

She scrawled a note. "Maybe we find it hard to imagine fighting from a planet. Maybe we should talk to some of the people who spent time waiting for us to rescue them." *From you.*

"I'll talk to one of the others about meeting with us," Kalin said. "We all experienced it differently. The whole team should be there if we can get someone to agree."

Why didn't he push back? Teamwork wouldn't give her the chance to take the credit she needed to rise when the new society started.

"You know, maybe I was wrong before. When I said I would have left the protesters to the security team. Maybe talking to them would be better."

"I don't think they want to listen."

The way he looked at her was perfect. He expected good advice, and he wouldn't know if she sent him down a path that made him look like a fool. And she would deny anything he said about her advice. She got the feeling he wouldn't justify his actions, simply take the fallout and move on.

"If it happens again, you should try to find the leader. Then you can ask about their motives. Maybe find a way to calm the situation."

He looked like he was considering the idea. He would be clumsy if he tried, and that would stir things up. Brianne was sure the people actually charged with stopping the protests could handle whatever damage Kalin caused.

"I'll think about it," he said, then stood. "I need a shower and a nap before the test. I left the report and completed checklist for installing the explosives in the drive. Your team can enter the details into the database."

He walked out, leaving her wondering again if she'd been played.

22

Kalin watched as the data rolled up the screen. The test had worked precisely as expected. Relief washed over him like a warm shower as the debris blossomed from the explosion. They got this right; there was hope for the whole plan.

After today, the range from the blast location would be too far to gather more information. The scouts speeding to their bases, losing contact with the drones. The drones dying one by one, so less and less data was arriving. He wasn't learning anything new but couldn't turn away from the screen.

"You need to get back to the weapon," Brianne said. "The analysts will go through all that. What do you hope to find, anyway?"

He told himself the snippy tone was in his imagination. His team, now working on the weapon, didn't need him leaning over them. At least his team was working. Brianne sat alone at her end of the table, Jim and Andor off on some mysterious mission for her again. He didn't care. What he wanted was to sit with Pen, drink a beer, and relax. The thought of days of staring at screens in hope of some revelation drained him.

Her question woke something inside, though. Yes, the roll of data hypnotized him, kept him looking, but she had a point; what did he expect to see? And everything on the display came from a delayed feed. The analysts saw the raw data. Should he ask for that to be sent here? Why? Knowing something a few seconds earlier wouldn't save them. The weapon needed to be ready.

"I don't know what I'm hoping to learn." He dragged his eyes away and moved toward his team. "Maybe something that tells us the enemy ship believed the ruse, that they think we're annihilated, and they are moving on to new prey."

"They are gone," she said. "For all we know, everything is fine and we can relax."

"Gone? Or hiding. We have no clue about their capabilities. For all we know they are following us just out of our sensor range. Or they discovered a way to hide their presence."

He watched as Mordecai scribbled a few notes on the schematic. Something about a sonic weapon for use on the planet. Beside the schematic, a drawing of sleek torpedoes hung with its own details. Explosives? Was there an armory on this ship? Or one of the others in the fleet?

"I thought you were the optimistic one." Brianne was beside him, looking over his shoulder. "That looks promising."

Mordecai looked up. "We found a bunch of information in an archive. The weapons techs are sorting through it. They've sent some stuff already. In space, we need to figure out how to enhance these torpedo things so they will move fast and far. If we wound the enemy, maybe we can escape."

"And they'll know how many ships we have," Brianne said. "Why harm them and not kill?"

Kalin scanned the full dataset on the screen. "Because we don't have a way yet to figure out how to destroy them. These are all guesses. Good ones, but we don't know their weaknesses."

"Yeah, and we want one kind of weapon," Elissa said. "If we split production into space and planet deployments, we weaken our position."

"If we had a view behind the debris," Wilma said, "I'd feel better. The enemy might be hidden by our own test results."

"We're about to hit speed," Brianne said. "Maybe if you had said something yesterday, a drone would be on the other side of that field."

And there it was again. Not so subtle this time. No one on the team seemed to recognize the insult in her words, or they didn't care. Maybe he should try that tactic. Let her do what she wanted and spend his energy keeping his team motivated.

"Good work," Kalin said. "Let's see if there's still a chance to put a drone through. I'll talk to the captain."

"That's my job," Brianne said.

"It's a big ask," Kalin said. "We'll do it together."

He might be willing to try ignoring her behavior, but this was too important to let her waste time twisting the idea. And he was sick of tiptoeing around her ego. If she thought he was ordering her around, too bad.

"Fine." Brianne sent an urgent meeting request to the captain.

Her pad responded in seconds. *Now. I'll come to you.*

Two minutes later, the captain walked through the door. "Make it fast."

Kalin outlined the request. "We think there is still time."

The captain made a call without answering them. Then he looked up from his pad. "They'll redirect the remaining drones to set a relay of feed from the other side. The scouts will extend the range by slowing their return."

"If the enemy is present, will they be safe?" Brianne asked. "I don't want to be responsible for any scouts being killed simply to satisfy curiosity."

"We have enough drones to be safe. If the enemy is able to locate us this far out, we are lost before we get a chance to fight." The captain checked the time. "I'll hold off on the acceleration for one hour. That should put the drones in place and still give the scouts time to join the last ship in the fleet. Not home yet, but as safe as we can make it."

He left them to turn back to the feeds. Now Kalin wanted the live feed. Now a few seconds might make the difference.

"Why didn't you tell him about the weapons progress?" Brianne said. "It's important for him to understand that we still need to finish a design."

"Write up the report and send it to him," Kalin said. "I think he's got enough on his mind getting the fleet ready."

"That is what happens when people leave things to the last minute. Someone should have thought of positioning the drones before we blew up *Tomorrow's Promise*."

She said it loud enough for the team members to hear, as if she was daring them to ignore her.

"We can't think of everything. The test was good," he said as loudly. "We know we can simulate it when we are on the planet. That was their focus, and they did great work."

Andor bustled into the room followed by Jim, both of them looking excited.

"You were right, lieutenant," Jim said. "The library

supervisor found a bunch of information when we asked the right questions."

Kalin looked at them, waiting for more information.

"Yeah," Andor said. "She said she'd send the link to the old battle records." He looked over to the team huddled over the weapons design. "Hey, we found you some help."

Elissa looked up from their work. "Yeah, we just got it. I had no idea we fought battles when we first left Earth."

Battles against the last ships to leave, my ancestors. "You were good at it too." He tried not to let the pain he felt come through in the words.

23

In the end, the captain had held back on starting the run for the planet until the morning. The information from the drones showed empty space behind the wreckage. Kalin expected relief, but all it left was the same worry that they'd missed something.

"This is the official start," the captain said. "From now on we are running, not exploring."

The captain and Whitnal's presences filled the room. The civilian leader was standing beside Brianne. The team spread out behind them. The screen showed the feed from the scouts. Not the sanitized one on the observation room walls, but the actual records. Kalin had his hand on the back of a chair to keep himself grounded as the views around him spun with dizzying speed. Everyone was doing the same. The radius of the test debris was moving slowly away from the center. The small gravitational pull of the drones and scout ships setting up chain reactions of pieces bumping into other pieces.

The feed started to settle as the drones destructed. Nothing to worry about; they didn't have enough power to make it back to the ships. It wasn't an attack. Vertigo released Kalin, and other people gave small gasps as the feeds lined up.

"Can we think of the flight as running for our home, rather than running away?" Brianne said. "It might be easier for people to accept."

"That is how we are framing our actions," Whitnal said. "No one will forget that we are fleeing an enemy we can't fight, but optimism is probably a better motivator than fear. Even the protesters can't battle too hard against finding our home."

Protests still plagued the fleet, not just *Dark Prospect*, but every ship had some group of dissatisfied people. Kalin had warned the team earlier to make sure no one followed them to the room. Their work was a blunt instrument, and sometimes brutal statistics lined the walls. There was no optimism here for anyone, even those involved in building the weapon.

"We are making progress," the captain said. "I'm meeting with the ringleaders once we're underway."

Whitnal chuckled. "Perhaps calling them concerned citizens would be less provocative than ringleaders."

"It's what they are," Brianne said. "Perhaps we need some security here. In case they find us."

The captain looked at her for a moment without speaking. Her idea was good, Kalin thought. But this wasn't the right time. He glanced around at the team. They appeared to be focused on the screens, but their attention seemed forced.

"Have there been any incidents?" the captain finally asked. "We can move you to a more secure location."

"Not yet," Brianne said. "I'll send you a recommendation later today."

The captain nodded.

"It's time," Whitnal said. "The scouts are close enough that we can increase speed. They'll be aboard before there's any effect."

In fact, the scout ships were going offline as they returned to their home bays. Kalin wondered where Jo was in the group. Was he coming back, or had they assigned him to another ship?

"The feed is breaking up," Brianne said. "We're almost out of range of the debris."

Only twenty scouts left. Half for *Dark Prospect*, half for the next ship down the line. The center of the debris was losing detail. The very edges only a fuzzy blur of light against the black of space.

"Fifteen minutes to final docking," a scout reported. "All drones now offline."

"Is this on all screens?" Brianne asked. "I mean the cleaned-up version. I don't think we want the entire population of the fleet reeling around dizzy."

"All the screens," Whitnal said. "And yes, only a few of us lucky ones got to experience the full force of so many inputs. I won't do that again."

Avoiding the vertigo would be a bonus, but not if they missed information. It would be a few more hours before they received any analysis to confirm they got what they wanted from the test. But everything was conjecture anyway. Watching didn't give them any insight, but it felt like they were doing something.

"Will there be a next time?" Kalin asked. "What is left for us to test?"

Brianne gave him a look behind the captain's back that made him feel like a fool.

"We can test weapons, or parts of them," she said.

The captain turned from the screen as three scouts shut down their feeds. It wouldn't be long before the screens would show nothing from the outside.

"We must take care with that," he said. "Our ability to produce the projectiles is not unlimited. And we must be cautious of leaving a trail of destruction for anyone to follow."

"We also are out of targets," Whitnal said. "Even if another ship or two need to be abandoned, we can't keep blowing them up, or leave them floating empty."

"An untested weapon is a risk," Kalin said. Brianne had a point, and so did the captain. Other targets could be made with some hard choices. What he didn't want was for Brianne to take out her frustration at being blocked on the whole team with snide remarks. "We should keep the option open."

"What will we do with any ships we need to evacuate?" Elissa asked. "I mean, just leaving them is as much of a trail to follow as destroying them."

"And there's another risk," Andor said. "We can't be sure any intelligence about our route, history, or weakness is removed. We could hand the enemy the key to our destruction. The plans we found from the early battles were clear about keeping intelligence locked down."

The captain gave another nod. "All good points. I'm not saying we simply leave the ship floating. I hope all ships will make it to our new home. If we must abandon one, then we can send it on auto-nav to a different section of space. Perhaps pulling the enemy away from our route."

"We'll think it through," Brianne said. "Give you some options."

Kalin had expected her to find a way to berate the team members who spoke out. Thank God Andor was on her team because that might be the only reason she didn't snap at everyone.

"One more question," Wilma said. He waited for the nod to continue. "Maybe we can come up with a name for our home? Wouldn't people feel more invested if we could call the planet something? Like we still call it Earth because it feels more personal than calling it our originating planet."

Whitnal turned to the captain. "Perhaps something we can ask the protest leaders to take on. Give them a bit of control. And if they come up with an unpopular idea, people won't use it and they can't blame us."

"Nice to have something other than weapons and battles on our minds. Good point, Ensign Castle."

"Oh shit." The voice came from one of the scouts.

Every head turned to the screen.

The center of the debris field bloomed toward them. In seconds, the sight of a silver ship broke through. A section of a sphere. The screen went blank.

The captain's pad buzzed. He read the message.

"The scouts have stopped transmitting to avoid any chance of detection. They will drop back and shelter on *Generation Humanity*."

24

B rianne waited for someone to speak but shock overtook the team. *Good, it gives me time.*

"We need to go back to working on the weapon immediately," she said. "We've run out of time to plan; we need to move into production."

"The ship stopped," the captain said. "We are still receiving some visuals. We don't know if the enemy has the capability to scan for us. And as little as we know about them, that could well be its rear bay."

"We can't wait to run," Lee Mukherjee said. "We can keep working on the weapon, but we need to speed up the fleet now."

"The order went out moments ago," Whitnal said.

"How long before we lose any chance of observing the enemy?" Wilma asked. "It's just as important to keep gathering information."

"*Far Spaces*," the captain said. "The last ship in the fleet. We'll have scouts from them do what they can without obviously drawing attention."

Brianne couldn't think of anything constructive to ask.

She was losing her moment. "The test probably gave them our location." As soon as the words were out, she knew she'd made a mistake. Wrong time to assign blame. The captain didn't even look at her. Whitnal narrowed his eyes. She thought he was an ally. Had she lost him? Maybe there was still a way to rescue the situation. "Of course we needed to do the test, just... we shouldn't do more, I guess; too risky."

"Thank you, lieutenant," the captain said, not looking at her. "We will continue to make those kinds of decisions with risk in mind when they arise."

"We need all the data live now," Kalin said. "The way the ship moved the debris might give us some idea of its size, or anything that reveals the material it's made of."

"Actually, the movement is more important," Lee said. "We can infer things like size, but then we can translate that to speed. Anything we can gather about repositioning right now would help. If the ship is stationary, it will give us more time. Maybe send a few drones?"

"Sure, maybe we should just tell them our location," Brianne said. "Every extra bit of data we gather means risking lives. And probably giving them everything they need to destroy all of us."

"I think we can balance out the risks, and we will ask for volunteers," the captain said. "Yes, it is risking lives, but many more are at risk if we don't learn as much as possible about the situation."

"We need to start on communications," Whitnal said. "At this point, the news is held close. It could leak on any of the other ships before Pen can craft the message."

"Kalin, please send any requests for data, or help, to my office within the hour. The window is closing for more observation." The captain nodded at Brianne and thanked the rest of the team for their hard work so far. "I have every confidence that you will succeed."

"We're getting more feed now," Kalin said. "I'll talk to the analysts too and find out what they cleaned out before sending the data to us. Maybe there's something in the gaps between the live feed and our cleaned version to help us."

The captain's pad buzzed, and he moved to the far corner to take the call. Roger Whitnal joined her at the table while he waited. "A word, lieutenant?"

She pushed her pad to the side and gave him her whole attention. If he had advice, it was an opportunity to gain his support. Being aligned with the civilians would help get her the power she wanted when they landed.

"You are charged with a difficult job," he said. "Being the Devil's Advocate tends to paint a person as a loner and someone who doesn't work well on a team."

He had it right. Not that she ever cared about playing well with others. She was usually right when she pointed out problems. "Thank you for noticing."

"You need to be careful."

Brianne expected to be given some congratulations on seeing problems before anything truly went wrong. Not this. "What do you mean?"

He kept his eyes on the captain as he spoke. "You want a role in the colony leadership, yes?"

She nodded.

"You will need people to vote for you. And to do that, you need a reputation for listening and caring. Your words matter."

Sure, words mattered. The difference between someone who got recognized and one who faded into the background was all about making sure your words hit home. She needed to make the captain believe she cared about people, not just results. "Was I wrong in saying we can't risk lives to maybe get some information that might help?"

The captain finished his call and headed toward Whitnal.

"The way you say it is far more important than what you say." He stood and joined the captain.

"We have some decisions to make," the captain said to Whitnal.

They moved away but Brianne caught part of their conversation as they approached the door.

"Plans to be ready to evacuate..." Whitnal was saying. The rest was lost as the door closed.

Another ship? Which one? They didn't have time to organize testing another decoy.

Kalin called her over to join in the discussion. Everyone was tossing in requests for information, materials, people to help. The lines between her team and his were gone. That couldn't continue. Sitting alone on her side of the table made Whitnal's words ring true. If he didn't think she deserved a position now, she couldn't let him see how she'd been pushed aside.

"What about sound?" she asked. Anything to offer a suggestion. "There must be something as the ship brushed against debris. Is there any way we could retrieve anything like that?"

Idiot. The sound would be so localized no one would dare approach close enough to catch it.

"If only one of the drones had been live when the ship appeared," Lee said. "If it recorded vibrations from the contact, we would have them."

Kalin noted it on the list. "It's worth asking. We don't know how slowly the ship moved. Maybe the final drones did transmit sound. Or maybe one of them got bumped and sent that data."

She refused to feel better about it. She needed them to accept her ideas without Kalin pointing out how good they were.

"Jim, Andor, we need to start prepping the list for the captain." She beckoned them away from the others. "In fact, Jim, go talk to the analysts and find out what they cleaned from the feeds. Asking in person might help focus the requests."

Kalin looked up from the work and thanked her. "It will save us a lot of time."

We'll see. I need to get us planet-side. That's where the future is. And if Whitnal says I have to play it differently, I'll figure it out.

25

Kalin stood with his team in the shuttle bay shelter, not willing to wait out the moments between landing and the outer doors sealing before they caught a glimpse of the ships. This time, two teams from security checked everyone who entered long before they could cause a problem. The shuttles were docked, and the space cleared for the scouts.

Over the last day as the fleet sped up, the pilots had been moving in silent mode. No transmission of information, no discussion between them.

Dark Prospect was going to shelter all the pilots for two days. Kalin's team wasn't the only one trying to squeeze every drop of information, provable or guessed at, but they were the first.

The entire team was in attendance. Brianne waited to the side, holding a recording device.

"Jo's going to be busy the next couple of days," Pen said. "I'm sure he can find some time to talk with you after all this is done."

Jo had been out with the scouts. Fully trained and now assigned to them for the duration, his training on other duties were stalled by the circumstances. "You think he might come up with some ideas? Something he won't say now?"

"The rest of the scouts are very good at observation. Since we started them roaming around, they've come up with some interesting insights. Jo? He's been in battle. The others haven't."

The battle was with me. He didn't acknowledge the cost of that experience aloud. Pen was right; Jo had a different perspective than the rest of his flight. "You think I should hold my people back? Wait until we can talk to him privately?"

She moved to stand beside him and touched his shoulder. "No, but remember they are exhausted. None of them will call an end to the questions, but you'll get more depth after a rest."

And his group of planners would have time to develop more questions. "Okay. I'll call the end when I see them flagging. When is their next session? Who with?"

"The captain gave them four hours after you finish to rest and visit their friends. Then, full back-to-back with the analysts, the weapons people, the archivists."

Kalin didn't envy the pilots. And he wouldn't make it worse by dragging out his time with them. "Are you hanging around?" Pen being here would be a good buffer between himself and Brianne. There was no way she was crazy enough to be confrontational with a witness like Pen. And, besides, he loved having her near enough to touch.

"Only long enough to say hi to Jo and then I need to head back. We're running a town hall today. Let people ask their questions, give everyone on the fleet a chance to feel included."

The alarm sounded and the blast doors slid closed behind the security personnel who were retreating for the main body of *Dark Prospect*.

He chuckled. Another task he didn't envy, managing people who should know better than to interrupt a briefing. "Think of it as practice. When we land, it's all going to be collaboration."

All the ships docked within a few minutes. Really, too close for safety under normal circumstances. The first door opened as soon as the alarm went silent, and gravity normalized. The pilot stepped out. Jo looked like he hadn't slept in a month, and at the same time as though he'd just won the lottery. That feeling Kalin understood.

Pen hurried over and hugged Jo, said a few words and then left with a wave to Kalin, ducking under the blast doors as they rose from the floor.

Jo tossed his helmet into the cockpit and strode over. "First victim reporting for duty."

Brianne moved closer. "We'll record the session," she said. "It will minimize the need to keep taking up your time."

Jo nodded and looked over to the cluster of people. "How do you want to do this?"

While they had Jo alone, it would be easy. Keep the questions controlled so they didn't all shout for answers at the same time. As soon as more ships opened, Kalin planned to break the groups up. He hoped the scouts were checking for maintenance concerns rather than staying inside because of injuries.

"Sit over there." He pointed to the table. Bottles of water

and a stack of sandwiches filled the center. "Just answer as best you can. If it gets too much, let me know."

Jo sat and started answering questions. Brianne moved closer to the table. "We should keep the group together," she said. "I'll arrange for individual sessions later."

He didn't understand how that would work; fifteen scouts headed their way. "We'll see how it goes."

She nodded and watched the questions.

"Can you tell what the orientation of the enemy ship is?"

"Any indication of sensors aimed this way?"

"Material. Can you guess at the composition of the ship's skin? It will help with weapon design."

"Was there damage to the ship?"

Jo did his best to answer but made sure it was clear when he was offering a guess and when he knew the answers. After about ten minutes the rest of the scout ships opened up, and the answers became more discussions. Each pilot checked for some kind of agreement from his colleagues before giving a guess.

Brianne had placed the camera on a tripod and joined Kalin.

"I didn't expect this to be so productive," she said. "Why aren't they falling asleep in their chairs?"

"Adrenaline. Watch carefully."

It started happening as the questions slowed. The first of the scouts started blinking rapidly. Another slumped in his chair and closed his eyes. Jo was pinching his thigh. Without stimulation, their exhaustion was taking over.

"I think that's enough," Kalin said, stepping toward the group. "We'll set up more time later."

Jo stood and tried to assist another pilot to his feet. He didn't have the strength to hold himself up.

"We'll help you," Brianne said. "Everyone, grab a pilot and support them as we head out."

Jo stepped back. "I can make it on my own."

Kalin beckoned to the head of the security team and then said, "You can't, and you are heading for medical. A nap and a drink of water isn't enough."

"If we go out leaning on the arm of an escort, everyone will suspect something is wrong." Jo reached out and tried to help the other pilot again.

The security head joined them.

"What's it like between here and the closest medical section?" Kalin asked.

The woman looked at the pilots and shook her head. "Too far to go without being noticed. We'll bring a medic and get them on their feet. Ten minutes, okay?"

"Thank you," Jo said and then sat back in the chair.

Brianne turned off the recorder. "No more questions, but did you want to tell us anything we haven't asked?"

"I do," one of the pilots said. "You probably want it on record."

Brianne turned the device back on and waited. Kalin couldn't quite accept this new side of her. Where had the caring come from? If she could keep it up, they'd be further ahead with the job.

"Tell us your name first," Brianne said.

"Ari Sloan. I don't know what this means, but I swear my drone feed blipped at the end. Did you notice it?"

"The feed went out," Kalin said, "but we still had the cleaned version. It might have made a difference."

"I think, maybe, that ship came to check what the explosion was about," Ari said. "The blip? It could have been them trying to read the memory. Good thing drones are short on storage space."

"We'll look at the raw feed," Kalin said. They would be able to find Ari's records easily. "That might tell a lot." Including that the ship wasn't looking for them until *Tomorrow's Promise* blew up. And if it did attract the enemy, had his test put them in more danger?

26

The raw data arrived on Brianne's terminal within the hour; now she had the opportunity to get an edge by seeing the problem first. Thankfully, they'd sent only the last fifteen minutes of the stream. The blip should be in there near the end, but it wasn't only the drone feed, so the file was huge. She found the blip within minutes. Almost the last thing on the feed and surrounded by scouts' comms.

She called Kalin over. "Look, the drone was almost dead by the time the blip happened."

"And it finished transmitting to us," he said, pointing to the size of the drive. "So even if the enemy destroyed the drone, they might not have any information."

"The breakdown happened as it was deleting the navigation history." No chance the drone could be identified from whatever remained in memory. "If the enemy targeted it, there's nothing leading to us."

"But the interruption is there," Kalin said. "We can't ignore it. Anything we get from that data is just a guess, and with any amount of information gathered, we might still be wrong."

True, but I can use any of this to be the good guy. Taking Whitnal's advice was going to be easy. And maybe, he'd see her adaptability and willingness to listen and change as an asset when the time came to creating a planet-based power structure.

"I'll send the captain our assessment," she said. The report would not include Kalin's name on anything that might look good. "What are you going to do with this?"

He looked at the team hunched over some printouts at the end of the table, Chan and Owusu discussing some point excitedly. "Take precautions. If this was a coincidence, then we may have given the enemy a big clue about us. If we assume the enemy took out the drone, that means they were nearby when the ship blew. Were sensors active at the time? Before we destroyed *Tomorrow's Promise*?"

"That is standard procedure," she said, "but there's no record of any hint the enemy was nearby. It's possible the commanders of the ship ignored the usual precautions in the rush to leave."

He shook his head. "The problem might not be the sensors. If the enemy ship can move fast, the sensors are definitely not strong enough. If they were out of range when the scouts and drones deployed, and then at the blast site, what, ten minutes later? We need to boost the signal. And do so without laying a trail to the fleet. We're going to burn ourselves out trying to cover every option."

He thinks everything is his fault. That the blast showed the enemy the location of the fleet.

"The ship hasn't moved," she said. "Maybe they were simply curious. Maybe your test worked."

He nodded, still watching his team. "And maybe we are

out of range unless we do something like the test again and catch their attention."

Brianne kept her smile from showing. That would be a nice tidbit for the report. Nothing direct, just a recommendation to avoid triggering more explosions.

"We need to change tactics," she said. Time to be helpful. "We need to extend the range of the sensors and the weapon. If we attack from far enough out, they can't respond."

"We hit them first?" he asked, finally turning his attention to her. "That sounds like your hunt and destroy strategy. The captain won't go for it."

He should.

"No. It's completely different. I'm saying we keep moving toward the planet. We attack if they appear in our sensors. We don't go looking for them. Maybe we'll lose them but if not..."

"Stronger sensors mean we risk leaving a trail." He glanced at the data again. "We might be too late. What about moving faster to the planet? What do you know about the fleet capability?"

"We're going at the speed of the slowest ship, nothing more. The captain figured it was enough." *Let him say abandon another one. The captain is already preparing anyway, but I need to stay out of the harsh recommendations for a while.*

"Who would be aware of each ship's capability?" he asked. "Not simply to speed up as is, but if a few repairs could give them the ability, we can make that happen. If we need to leave more ships, it makes more sense not to stretch things out. Multiple disasters will leave a trail."

"I can find out, but this isn't our job, right? Why don't I put a recommendation in this report? Maybe analyzing the effect of bringing the population on to the four fastest ships?"

"If there's room. I mean we only need a few ships to set a diversion when we arrive. There are plenty of supplies on four ships to start a colony." He glanced at the team again. "Ask for resources, too. Weapons specialist, communications techs. Asher Jones."

"We don't need a spy," she said. *And I don't need someone on the team who sees through my plans.*

"I was thinking deception tactics might help. He's working on dealing with the protests, but maybe he can give us a day."

"I'll ask for an expert in deception tactics, then. He might not be the best. And what about an encryption specialist?"

"You think if we code the data being sent to us, it will help? I'm worried about the direction of the information, not the content."

And that's why I'll be the hero in the end. "If the data can be disguised as regular noise, there's no reason for anyone to follow it. I'm sure the experts can come up with more ideas."

"Whatever you think. I'll split the team to focus on different tactics. Speed is probably outside our mandate, but we should be ready to take it on. The weapon, we can definitely build a boost into the specs. And I'll work with them. The rest can work with the comm tech to develop the tracking stuff. We might still have a chance."

He left her to join the group still huddled over a pile of specs. She sent Andor out to find out about the capability of each ship in the fleet. If they couldn't dump the slow ones, deploying the weapon should include all the ships, and the way to find the enemy. So, if the weapon was going to the last ship in line, she was going with it.

She sent off the report with its clear indications that while the whole team was working on the problem, the new suggestions came from her.

27

Kalin waited for the captain to speak. It had been two days since the enemy ship appeared. Two days since the fleet sped up. The plans for deploying the weapon were moving along. But it was also two days of less-than-optimal speed.

The captain had called them in for a briefing. Brianne stood beside him apparently patient while Whitnal and the captain finished a conversation.

"I'd like a report on progress," the captain said as he turned to include them in the discussion. "Nothing formal, just where you are with the weapon and how long before you can make the thing operational."

There was something going on. If he wanted a quick update, he didn't need to call them in.

"The weapon should be operational within the next couple of weeks. We've done some virtual testing of components. Of course, we don't have a way to test it completely."

"And if you needed to deploy before that timeline?" Whitnal asked. "What's your best guess at success?"

"The weapon will fire," Brianne said. "Whether it will be

fully effective is another question. And the range is too short for safety. In essence, we can aim and shoot, but not far and possibly not effective enough if by chance we hit the enemy. And we risk being caught in the destruction field if we don't have more range."

The captain and Whitnal exchanged glances. The civilian leader nodded and motioned for the captain to tell them.

"The enemy ship has started moving," the captain said. "Slowly. We are still gaining distance, but it's moving in our direction."

Brianne stiffened. "There's no guarantee we can deploy the weapon from this distance."

"I understand," the captain said. "We are not sure if the change is an indication that they are following us, or just repositioning."

Too many uncertainties for comfort. "I suggest we move faster," Kalin said. "If we abandon *Far Spaces*, we can increase our speed by forty percent."

"And there we have the other problem," Whitnal said. "The protesters are active again. It appears a little participation in decisions isn't enough. They know we could go faster. They don't want us to overcrowd."

"Letting them stand in the way of saving the fleet is dangerous." Kalin couldn't keep his frustration inside. Now that he could answer back, respectfully, he would do so. "We should evacuate the ship and send it off in the opposite direction. A little overcrowding is nothing compared to death."

"It's not that easy," Brianne said. "Overcrowding will breed more dissatisfaction. I'm sure they aren't trying to put us in danger. They feel like no one listens, and that can be hard to accept."

Whitnal looked impressed. "Yes. And if the protest turns to rebellion, we won't be able to focus on the external threats."

"That's why we are here," the captain said. "This meeting is private; we are able to discuss difficult choices. Whatever is said in here, it stays between us. Your weapon is the key. We need to tell people we are able to fight."

And give them a chance to argue about that? As a distraction?

"How can you be sure telling them will help?" Kalin asked. "These rebels are happy to question every decision. Having them weigh in on the design and deployment seems foolhardy."

"But each time we give them a little say, more concerned citizens stop rebelling. The plan is good even if it simply divides them," Whitnal said. "None of us is experienced in quelling a rebellion. And I don't think we want to gain any skills in that discipline. Please don't call them rebels; they are protesters, or concerned citizens, or anything other than actual rebels."

Kalin felt Brianne shift beside him. He prepared for her to argue with his recommendation. Over the last two days, that was her tactic. Anything he suggested, she would propose the opposite despite doing so meant she changed her mind from one moment to the next. Dealing with his own protester was hard enough.

"Are you still meeting with the leaders?" she asked.

"Yes, they are still involved in briefings. We still ask for their input," Whitnal said.

"Put them in charge of the evacuation," she said. "Maybe giving them something to do will shut them up for a while. If Kalin is right about the fleet capability, won't we be on the planet in less than two weeks?"

"You would put people who disagree with the decision

in charge of the execution?" Kalin would never understand these people. First, they had the stupidity to argue against plans that gave them a chance of survival, and then the leaders want them to be responsible for making it work.

The captain held up his hand to stop the discussion. "Thank you for that suggestion, lieutenant. How would you implement it? I don't trust them to change so radically. Kalin is right that we have no choice about *Far Spaces*, and it might not be the last ship we lose."

"Not my area of expertise," Brianne said. "I would give them the consequences too, and the authority to move people around. If all ships took some of the complement, we should be fine. It's only for a few weeks anyway. And do a big announcement about how they are helping to save all of us. Maybe they want credit for a solution and then they'll quiet down. No one will want to face the backlash if they don't succeed. Tell people we developed a weapon. I'm sure Pen will know how to word it."

"We could ensure them a voice in the planetary governance, too." Whitnal shrugged. "I guess, not a voice, but a place. If they can earn the votes. I'll talk to Asher about it. He's been observing the leaders of these protests."

That is a problem for later. Kalin had no plans to be responsible for anyone other than himself and maybe Pen if she still wanted him when they landed.

"How long will it take to do this?" he asked. "The longer we wait, the more we need to rush the weapon. If the enemy is coming after us, we need to be ready."

"We'll convene the other captains and civilian leaders," the captain said. "Including the protest leaders, perhaps we can think of them as civilian leaders too. Tomorrow morning. We won't break until we sign off on an agreement. The evacuation can start later in the day. We could be up to speed in forty-eight hours."

"And the other ships? The ones you think we'll need to evacuate?" Kalin didn't want to go through this delay again. "Should we do it all at once?"

The captain picked up his pad and opened a message. "We might not need to do this again. The uncertainty isn't that the other ships can't achieve speed; they all have the ability. We worry that some will not be able to maintain at high levels for long enough. The only ship we can be sure of is our own, and that is too small for everyone. Thank you for your honesty. I hope to hear more good news about the weapon soon."

28

Do they know someone is observing? Kalin turned to ask Brianne the question, but her eyes glowed, and she'd never smiled so broadly before. Spying on the leaders' meeting made him uncomfortable, but she seemed to be enjoying every second.

The door to the small room opened and Asher stepped in. "First time?" he asked, nodding to the screen.

"I had no idea this existed," Kalin said. "Does someone spy on every meeting?"

Brianne didn't acknowledge the conversation. Her focus was tight on the screen, so perhaps she was unaware of it.

"I don't think so. This room is the only one where the meeting is piped in. Usually, a meeting isn't even recorded."

"Are you here for Whitnal?"

Asher glanced at the screen where the civilian leader sat next to the captain, not with his peers.

"I'm off to *Far Spaces*. Pen and I are facilitating the evacuation with the assigned leaders, or will be as soon as the decision is announced and they are out of the room."

"Then why are you here?" The decision wouldn't be fast,

but Kalin imagined a fair amount of preparation needed to be done. "You should be on your way."

"I had a talk with Ensign Mukherjee. She'll work with my friends in encryption. Good idea to mask information that way."

"My idea," Brianne said, not taking her eyes off the action. "Glad you agree."

"Mukherjee is meeting with them as we speak," Asher said. "Tell me how it goes. I think we'll all work together more in the future. I need to know how my team members fit in with people in the world outside our little enclave of secrets."

The sound from the screen turned from rustling and murmuring of people settling, to silence.

"I will," Kalin said.

"Talk to you when I get back." Asher pushed through the door.

"The protest leaders are all clumped together," Brianne said. "They shouldn't be allowed to do that."

The meeting was being held in an auditorium. The captain, Whitnal and a couple of military officers stood at the front. The rest of the participants sat waiting. It wasn't a large group. Twelve captains, twelve civilian leaders. Some of those were newly appointed. Before the fleet joined up, the military ran most ships. Four of the captains sat with their civilian counterparts, the others clumped in groups of two or three. The four leaders of the protesters sat together distanced from the others as Brianne noted.

"Too soon for them to feel part of anything," Kalin said. "It's odd that all the leaders are in one room."

"You think someone will take advantage?" She finally turned from the screen to look at him.

"If someone was planning to, the captain has given the

opportunity," Kalin said. "But the two security guys up front might be there to prevent an attempt at a takeover."

"No one would," Brianne said.

"A week ago, no one thought people would protest."

She turned back to the screen. "Yes. Why don't people just do the right thing until we leave space for a planet?"

Ignoring the comment, Kalin watched the cluster of troublemakers. They paid attention, but when the captain stopped speaking, they started a quiet conversation.

A tall older man stood, and for a moment, Kalin thought he was going to walk out.

"What if people refuse to move?" the tall man asked. "You plan to lock them up?"

"We will persuade them," Whitnal said. "It is important that this action be completed quickly to make the most of our ability to run."

"The people on my ship will cooperate." The captain of *Far Spaces* looked up at the man. "We expected it."

"All of them?" the tall man asked. "You didn't need to force anyone? I find that hard to believe."

The civilian leader of *Far Spaces* stood and faced the protester. "You are right. Some people were reluctant, but we did nothing to force anyone. This is for the good of the fleet. We'll all be abandoning our ships soon enough. Len, if you'd taken up the offer to organize this, you would be aware of the details."

"And if someone changes their mind? Will you arrest them?"

What was this man doing? Did he instruct people to go about stirring up problems? Or was he trying to get on record as the defender of individual rights in the face of attack and death?

The captain took control of the discussion. "Len, what

would you suggest we do? I'm sure people can be influenced to resist leaving their homes, but if they do, we are left with very few options."

"I'm not convinced this enemy is heading our way. The ship we see could be one of Kalin's people. The destruction of his ship might have been an accident. We've been given no proof we are in danger. When you consolidate the population, you increase your power." Len's voice rose as he got further from any sensible ideas.

"The plan is to spread the complement of *Far Spaces* through the fleet," Whitnal said. "Their leaders will remain in that position. They will have equal representation. As though they are on a virtual ship."

"We could repair the problem," Len said.

Kalin noticed his companions drawing away as he balked at the plan.

"Not in time," the captain said. "You had no objections earlier when I spoke to you. What's changed?"

Len checked the people sitting around him. No one made eye contact.

"I thought this was the forum for that," he said when no one stepped up to join him. "You say we are part of the process, but you tell us what you plan and expect us to simply fall in line."

"We expect people to see the need," the captain said. "The fleet needs to move faster. *Far Spaces* is not equipped to do that. You are not convinced of the threat, but I have offered to show you the proof and you refused. What is the alternative?"

"Coming up with solutions is not our job," Len said. "I will keep listening to the people who agree that our freedoms are being thrown away."

"Does he believe what he said?" Kalin asked. "That there is no threat?"

Brianne shook her head. "I don't understand how he's come up with the idea, but he's sticking to it. And it doesn't matter if he believes it; he'll use it to cause problems. They should shut him down and lock him up."

"Someone else will just start up," Kalin said. "What freedoms is he talking about?"

She laughed. "None. We've never had much freedom because we rely on the ships running well to survive. We don't suffer under a dictatorship, but the military is in charge. He's talking about taking away something that will only exist when we land and have a planet to develop."

The meeting was breaking up on the screen. Whatever this Len guy thought, the captain had managed to gain agreement from everyone.

So far, every tactic they tried had worked, and Brianne was running out of time. In the week since *Far Spaces* went off on autopilot to some random system, Kalin and his team finished the weapon design and were halfway to building it. And they had a great solution, except for the fact they couldn't test a single component.

A pulse weapon that can only be used once wasn't a complete success. When they landed on the planet, they might find out it would work more than once. They can recharge, but no one knew how long that would take because it was another thing they couldn't test, and some of the components were too rare to waste.

"Are you ready to make the presentation?" she asked Kalin. She'd tried to be gracious when she suggested he present the solution, and the effort paid off. Now if it was a failure, she was clear of any blame. If he succeeded? Well, she had all kinds of experience taking credit without doing the work.

"There isn't much to tell," he said. "The captain already

knows everything, and the last few improvements didn't make a significant change."

How could he be so oblivious to the political side of things? When they settled, he'd disappear into a role like farmer or shopkeeper. Good, less competition.

"This isn't for the captain. Or, not for what you think. People are restless again. We've seen no sign of the enemy ship for days. We're okay on *Dark Prospect*, but crowding is a problem on *The Orchard,* and supplies are low on *Generation Humanity*. Without the obvious threat, people are going to start causing problems."

He shrugged, like he didn't care. Like problems on other ships wouldn't affect them. Like a mutiny this close to their new home wouldn't be a disaster.

"Our job is to ready the weapon for deployment. We're almost done. The other stuff? Whitnal's problem. The military isn't going to turn on the captain."

A big part of Brianne wanted to explain reality to Kalin. To point him to the histories she found about food riots and just plain violent protest on old Earth. That wouldn't help though. She listened to the small voice inside that made sense to her. The worst wouldn't happen. In a few days people would be heading down to a planet. In a few days, they'd be too busy figuring out how to survive to spend energy on rebelling. Let Kalin look the fool. You have no obligation to educate him.

"I suppose," she said. "I mean, he was right about finding a name for the planet. The whole voting and choosing process kept people occupied for a few days. I guess it was always going to be some ancient deity's name that won."

She privately thought Damu was an odd name, but better than Home of Light and Hope.

"If this isn't only about the weapon, what do I need to do in the meeting?" Kalin tapped his pad, and the wall screen showed a diagram of the weapon.

"No one wants that much detail," she said. "And it's only us, the captain, and Whitnal. They want the strategy, not the specs. They want to be able to reassure people, put off the grumbling for a few more days. Something to quiet that Len guy and his crazy followers."

He started flicking through slide after slide of detailed notes. She tried to ignore the urge to grab his pad and type up speaking points. Being in the room when he stumbled through a lame presentation was going to be painful. And it might damage her too if either Whitnal or the captain wondered why she didn't speak. So she had to make sure he got the minimum points covered right.

"It's three areas," she said with a sigh. "Will the weapon work? Can we be sure? What do we tell people?"

"Telling people is Pen's job," he said. Then he held up his hand to stop her telling him why it was his job. "I know. We need to give her the details so she can make the news palatable."

"So, will it work?"

"I think so," Kalin said. "Without a test, we can't be sure. And even with a test, we are guessing because we don't have a spare enemy to use."

Wimp. How did a killer turn out this wishy washy?

"That adds another point. How does the weapon work? Pen will need that information to explain the risks. Telling people 'we don't know' isn't going to satisfy them; it will make the problem worse."

"A pulse beam. Able to go through space and through an atmosphere without exploding the air. At least, one that we can live in. If the weapon works, we are prepared to attack no matter where we meet the enemy. The beam will disrupt the structure of the ship, and it will disintegrate."

Better than 'we don't know' and maybe no one would ask what happens if this enemy boards the ship, or lands on the planet.

"She can work with that. And what about the whole strategy? It's not just blowing up the ship. Not meeting the enemy is better, right?" Not a battle she had any chance of winning, so no point in bringing up going on the offensive again. "Don't expect that people will put everything together without help."

"Okay. I can remind people about the decoy." He started typing on his pad.

"What if it's not just the four of us?" Brianne said. She couldn't let him blow the whole thing, but it would help her if he was nervous. And she knew this inside out—she could always take over if he stumbled.

"The captain would let us know if he invited someone else." He kept his eyes on his pad, but she heard uncertainty in his words.

"He might not get a chance. The meeting is in an hour." That should increase his anxiety. It would be even better if one of the protest leaders was in the room, but she wouldn't get away with inviting anyone.

"Thanks, Brianne," Kalin said. "I guess I still don't understand how things really work when 'just follow orders' isn't the rule."

She leaned over his shoulder and suggested changes as he wrote, even where he didn't need help. This was her area of expertise. Making people uncomfortable while offering to help. The skill had gotten her this far, had put her in front of the important leaders. The other ships might have their own captains and civilian leaders, but *Dark Prospect* was the head of the fleet, and the other ships did as her captain ordered.

30

The weapon looked complete on the screen. Kalin was glad he'd taken Brianne's advice. If anyone wanted the detailed drawings and specs, they could ask for them. The image drew everyone's attention. Better on the screen than on him.

The black cylinder telescoped to twice its size when he pressed a button on the remote. Then it moved to show all angles. Time to start talking.

"It's almost complete," he said. "The final casing is currently being manufactured. We expect to be ready by tomorrow."

"The scale?" Whitnal asked. "How do we deploy?"

Kalin pressed the button again and a human figure appeared. As the weapon turned to stand on its end, an arrow slid in to indicate the weapon stood about twice as long as an average adult. "It is heavy but can be carried by two people for a short distance. The mounting won't fit on a scout ship, and we can't deploy with drones. One of the shuttles is being fitted to allow us to deploy in space if needed. On land, the shuttle is modified to anchor into anything we encounter."

"If we were able to test it, I'd be happier," Brianne said.

The captain nodded at her comment. "No point in wishing for something we can't have."

"What's the full plan," Whitnal asked, "assuming we reach Damu before we need to deploy?"

"We developed two plans," Kalin said. "Will you announce them to the general populace?" He did understand the need to make people feel confident in their survival, but every instinct said to keep this a secret, and he couldn't explain why.

"The protests are under control for now," Whitnal said. "The situation won't last if they find out we aren't being open. And someone will slip. The techs on the shuttle retrofit, anyone in the supply chain for the weapon components. We need to explain. We'll be in orbit in a couple of days. The ship isn't trying to catch up but is still moving toward us."

"I think both plans should be shared," Brianne said. "The protesters at least will ask questions. If you want to show you are open and honest, you can't hold back."

It is the captain's decision. Kalin wondered what Brianne was trying to do. All along she'd been adamant in the planning room that everything should be kept secret. If anyone found out their plans, they could make it very difficult to progress. Everyone would want to add their ideas and confuse the goal with their agendas.

Kalin reminded himself his duty was to give the captain and civilian leader the information and let them decide what to publish.

"Our plan for an attack in space is to mount the weapon in the shuttle as soon as it is ready. If we need to, because the enemy confronts us, or opportunity arises to surprise them before we reach Damu, then we are ready to go. If we do discharge, the shuttle will leave *Dark Prospect* and jettison the empty shell of the weapon before returning."

He waited. Brianne's advice. *Don't rush everything out at once. Give them time to think.*

She spoke first. "In that case, we should make sure we are ready to fire at a moment's notice."

Why does she keep trying to make that point? "We researched the battle plans from the beginning of this journey. It was clear not every plan should start with fire the first shot."

The captain looked down at the table. "I think we'll keep the location of the shuttle a secret," he said. "I don't think anyone will sabotage the weapon, but an accidental firing aboard ship will do the enemy's work for them."

"When are you passing on the information?" Brianne asked. "Would it be better to wait until the weapon is installed?"

"Roger was right that the protesters are under control, but they are getting restless. People know the enemy is there, no matter how much we wanted that held back, word got out. So they need to hear we are prepared."

"We'll wait until the shuttle is fitted, Lieutenant Stonehouse," Whitnal said. "Or tomorrow morning. Is there a reason you don't want us to share?"

Brianne looked to Kalin, like she thought he would answer. He couldn't help her. Yes, he didn't want to tell civilians about military operations, but he couldn't articulate why because it was instinct, and his instincts were all built in a different environment.

"I think about those stupid girls," Brianne said. "What if there are others who think the same way they did? Or anyone who thought maybe winning a fight would scare off the enemy permanently, even if we didn't manage to destroy them? Or any other unreasonable idea someone might use to take the weapon."

"We have taken measures to restrict communications to within the fleet," the captain said. "Your plan for after we land? Is there any other detail we can consider?"

Kalin changed the image on the screen. "The broad strokes are the same. We land, we find or make cover. We strip the ships of as much as we can. We enact the decoy."

"I must admit the decoy part makes me nervous," Whitnal said. "People are highly emotional about moving out of ships. How are they going to react to us destroying the entire fleet for a decoy rather than using the resources for the colony? Not that we could board and go anywhere else with this threat. But it's like the old-world explorers burning their ships."

"Pen will deal with that," the captain said. "I'm not immune to the fear of the finality we create with that action, but as you say, we can't do anything but colonize. So, using the ships as decoys makes sense."

"We'll need a location," Kalin said. "Can the navigators pinpoint a nearby system to destroy the fleet? Something just within the scout ship's range?"

"We'll be ready to input the coordinates as soon as we arrive," the captain said. "The actual location of Damu will still be a secret. People might not try to contact the enemy, but they will certainly try to position themselves for power on the new planet."

"Yes," Whitnal said. "We must be careful the transfer of power is controlled. It would be nice if we had a few years before the infighting and power games start."

He looked at Brianne as he spoke.

"Yes, we need to be careful who takes the leadership," Brianne said. "Until we know what dangers exist, order is important to keep us safe."

The meeting seemed to be over, but no one was calling an end. Kalin needed to get back to work. "If that's all, we should leave you to it," he said. "The team worked long hours to get us here. I recommend they be recognized for the effort."

"They will be," the captain said, "when we are on Damu. We've managed to keep their identities confidential up to now so they can concentrate on the job. When we are safe, they will be listed among the heroes of the journey."

31

A sound came from the captain's pad. Not loud, but definitely not the normal sound. It set Kalin's teeth on edge. The sound echoed in Whitnal's pad.

The captain looked at the screen.

"The scouts went dark."

What scouts? They are all in their bays. The fleet is sticking together, and the only movement between ships is emergency supply shuttles.

"All of them?" Brianne asked. "When?"

"Yes, all," Whitnal said. "We sent them out to keep launching drones and gathering data. That's how we learned the enemy is behind us."

Jo was one of the scouts.

"Sit," the captain said. "We need to think."

Kalin closed the images on the wall screen and joined Brianne at the table.

"No one else knows," the captain said. "At least for now. We can't keep this quiet. The scouts all have family and friends who will notice their absence."

Pen should know, and I'll tell her if no one else will. Her job and our relationship demand it. And Asher, and the officer in charge of the scouts. Yes, this is going to be open knowledge before we find answers. "Is there anything to suggest what happened?" He hoped for communications failure rather than the worst.

"Drones," Brianne said. "We must have some left to send."

"Already in process. It's never happened before, but it is a dangerous job. A number of contingency plans are in place. Your suggestions, please." The captain slipped back into his commander role so easily, Kalin wondered if the other collaborative persona was real or simply a means to getting his way.

"We need information to target the weapon," Brianne said. "If this was the enemy attacking, we need to fight. We can't wait for them to start the battle."

"We shouldn't use up our only defense without knowing for sure this is the enemy," Kalin said. This was a familiar territory for him, battle tactics, real experience, not just from histories. "We only get one chance to deploy."

"And if we wait, we may not get another chance to do anything," she said. "The weapon is meant to be used. We should use it."

"Kalin is correct," the captain said. "We must be very sure of the need. What else?"

"When will we obtain more information on the event?" Whitnal asked. "I know you aren't happy to take action based on a guess. We need to consider what to tell the fleet. Every leader received that alert."

Why did they think this was still a secret? Too many people had access to the knowledge, and it was devastating. People would react in shock, and not well. "We tell people what we know," he said. "And fast, before we lose the chance to control the message."

"Pen will take care of the communication," the captain said. "I don't want to panic people. It is possible this is a communications break, and the scouts will arrive at a docking bay."

"How long before we stop expecting that?" Whitnal asked. "We can't wait around. We need to get to Damu."

"We need to travel faster, if possible," Kalin said. "Do the scouts know where to go? Do they have the range to join us if we don't wait?"

The captain's pad chirped. "The drones we sent out to look are offline."

"Then it's not likely to be an accident," Kalin said. "How much more speed can we achieve?"

"If it's more likely to be the enemy, we need to fight," Brianne said. "How are you going to explain us abandoning the scouts? What do you think those protesters are going to do if we don't deploy a weapon when we've built one?"

"Check your tone, lieutenant," the captain said. "If we act on your impulse, we risk killing any surviving scouts. I am not asking you to make a decision. I want recommendations. Your team has been working on this problem for weeks. I assume your perspective on the situation is different from the other officers. If you have no suggestions, you can return to duty and await orders."

Her face tightened. Kalin couldn't believe she would argue with the captain. If she was as ambitious as everyone said, she should stop before she said something she couldn't come back from.

Brianne set her mouth and with a glance at Whitnal, who looked away, she said, "No, sir. Only what I already stated."

This wasn't how Kalin would leave things. If they walked away now, these two powerful men would think them unprofessional. That could spill over to his team. The people who had worked non-stop since the test to design and build the only thing that might save the fleet. He no longer cared about placating Brianne.

"You have our suggestions, sir. If I might add a few more points?"

The captain nodded.

"This is about what we say as much as about what we do. No matter how the others react to the decision, we need to stand firm. If we fight and hope any scouts still alive can find a safe way back to us, surely no one will argue against saving our people. If we leave? Well, the scouts will be lost, and that is a hard choice. People will be angry for a while. But it will not affect our original plan. The scouts had no specific role planet side. We can get to Damu and strip the ships. We can send the empty fleet off with shuttle pilots who can make their way back. The weapon will still be available if we need to fight on the planet."

"Good points," Whitnal said. "I don't think we have a choice. We run for the planet."

"There is one more thing," Kalin said. "If we assume this was a failure in systems, or that the enemy took out the scouts, they are lost. Without navigation and comms, the scouts cannot find their way back. But if they can navigate, do they know where to go? And can we be sure they have the power to make the journey?"

"If they can still navigate, they have the information they need to come," the captain said. "We provided the coordinates and each scout memorized them. If it is the enemy, we don't need to worry about them learning the location since their tactic appears to be blow everyone up first."

"You should make sure the communication includes that," he said. "If people think there's hope the scouts will join us, then they are less likely to disrupt the plan."

"I will make sure that happens," Whitnal said. "The civilians aren't used to losing people. The military may be trained to do so, but they haven't experienced it. I think theoretical skills gained through the simulations will be enough to buy us some time."

"Go back to the team," the captain said, nodding. "Don't tell them anything. The communication will be set for tomorrow morning to give Pen time to come back and do what we need. If word gets out, we'll deal with whatever that means. That gives Pen time to work, and possibly the scouts will find a way to contact us before we set the fleet in mourning."

32

Kalin stood in the observation room, staring at the screens. When he'd first come aboard, he would sit for hours hoping to see a glimpse of *The Righteous Storm*. That hadn't happened, but it was still a good place to think without interruptions.

The screens forming the outer wall of the room displayed the usual black with a few near objects. The stars farther out shifted to red due to the increased speed of the fleet. He wondered if the images were simply a recorded loop now. Perhaps cameras outside the ship fed images to replace the scout feeds. Surely, they couldn't risk anyone seeing a trace of the enemy. Or knowing the scouts weren't transmitting.

Three hours had passed since the meeting. The strain of waiting for the news to leak was a surprise to Kalin. He expected that it would get out and they'd be facing a rebellion given the protests, and maybe it would come, but for now the secret was still kept.

"I thought I'd find you here." Pen slumped into the next

seat. "I hate this. Waiting and imagining all kinds of awful things. People are going to be scared and angry."

"You know how to talk to them," Kalin said, leaning in and kissing her cheek. "It won't be that bad. The captain will keep things under control."

She leaned into him, and he put his arm around her shoulders. "I gave him my first draft. Nothing to do now until he calls me. Nothing except worry."

"About Jo?"

"I know it's not useful. But he's my friend. And I have every confidence he can take care of himself. If he has a chance to. I can handle how I feel when I'm distracted by work, but if I ever slow down..."

Yes, if the enemy hadn't destroyed the scouts, Jo would find a way back and Pen wouldn't need to handle anything. "We could steal a shuttle and go looking."

She snuggled closer. "Imagine how mad Jo would be if we did that. Plus, the drones didn't fare well."

They sat together for a while, Kalin feeling more peace with Pen beside him. Over the last week, they'd found a little time to discuss their feelings. Something the old Kalin would never be able to imagine doing. Whether their attraction was real or simply a reaction to the danger, they decided it didn't matter. They would deal with whatever happened when the danger disappeared, and simply enjoy the time they had now.

"Yeah. And he'd yell at you, forcing me to come to your rescue." He squeezed her shoulder to stop the giggles. "Do you not see me as the hero of old stories? Saving maidens, slaying dragons?"

She was laughing so hard she couldn't answer. A moment of release for both of them. Kalin stared at the screens again. No change.

"I told the captain not to wait," she said. "He should tell people now. I don't think anyone will care that we don't have all the answers."

"Why do you think no one knows yet? There are a lot of people involved. Scouts should have been arriving back by now. Their absence is going to be noticed."

She moved out of his arms and looked around the room. Kalin knew they were alone, but she waited to speak until she was sure.

"Because most of the people who know are military. They are under orders not to discuss it while the officers are working out a solution. The few civilians are not going to risk starting a mutiny or look like they've joined Les in his grumbling. And knowing won't make anything better."

"I can't be sure how long orders will work," Kalin said. "Your military is pretty lax."

She gave him the raised eyebrow look he recognized. "Okay, our military. Just because I'm part of it doesn't mean I understand."

"What would you do on your old ship in these circumstances?"

"We followed orders. My companions on that damn planet left me there on orders. My ship stranded me there on orders. Not only would we not be told about something like this, but we would also have been lied to. Told something about martyrs to the future, or heroes of the battle for righteousness."

"I can't say we won't lie. If the news gets out before the captain announces it, he might need to lie about what happened, what we know, and why we waited. "

"I just wish he would do it, so the waiting would end. The best thing right now would be for the scouts to appear. No message, no extra worry."

"Sitting here isn't helping." She stood and held out her hand. "Come on, show me your new weapon."

"We can't yet. The manufacturing process is classified, even from me. I can show you the shuttle we're adapting."

"Ooh, so romantic. Yes, show me your special shuttle. Maybe I'll come up with a way to get the captain to talk about it when he makes the announcement. People need hope that we can survive. I want to talk to your team members, too."

The shadow of worry didn't leave him as they walked away from the screens, but anxiety wasn't the only thing he felt now. Optimism was contagious.

"When we land on Damu, we'll gain a whole new set of things to worry about," Pen said. "I hope one of the problems isn't acid-spitting lizards, or homicidal trees."

This time he laughed. "Or endless cave systems that all look the same."

When they got to the shuttle bay, Kalin led Pen to the far corner next to the open blast doors. A temporary barrier hid the work on the shuttle. A guard stood at the entrance. She nodded them through without taking her eyes off the approach.

Kalin greeted the supervisor and introduced Pen. "Anything new?"

"Got orders to speed up. Should be done by tonight. You gonna have the device ready by then?"

Kalin checked the schedule on his pad. "No, but not much later."

Pen wandered around the workers assessing the modifications. Kalin watched her come to the realization of the size of the weapon. It was smaller than anyone had expected at the beginning. He joined her inside.

"We'll anchor the weapon here," he said, pointing to the large cross braces. "The rails are to allow a kick back."

"I thought it was a beam?" She ran her hands over the structure. "Why a kick back?"

"It's a pulse, so we anticipate some reaction. The shuttle will be on full gravity; the techs thought we would be safer than having zero g."

"And when we land?" She stood back, taking in the whole structure. "We won't have time to rebuild this."

"The shuttle will be anchored into the ground and move enough to aim. Less than an hour, the designers say. Of course, that's depending on what kind of land we're working with on Damu."

33

There wasn't much for the team to do until the weapon was ready. After the pressure of the last few weeks, it was hard for any of them to just stop. Kalin invited Pen to the strategy room to talk to whoever was working. After she'd talked to them, he'd send everyone home with orders to rest and relax until the next day.

He didn't want to admit how hard he had to work to be with the people he'd come to think of as friends and keep this secret.

Pen made him stop along the way to find beer and snacks. "Food helps to disconnect people from work. Trust me. You can't simply order them to relax; you need to show them what that means."

Pen pushed open the door and Kalin heard Brianne's voice. "Do you really think you know better?"

Inside the room were Brianne and her two team members, Jim and Andor, huddled around a pad, his own team in the process of removing the papers they'd had on the wall during design.

"Hey," Pen said. "I thought you'd like a celebratory

drink." She pointed at Kalin, and he put the box of treats on the table.

"Thanks," Wilma said. "It's kind of depressing cleaning up."

Kalin handed him a beer and took three to Brianne. "What are you finishing?" He tried to sound interested, but his suspicion came through — maybe only to him.

Andor looked up from the pad. "Communications," he said. "I think maybe someone is hacking the stream."

So, Brianne hadn't told them about the scouts. He called Pen over. "What makes you think your comms are being hacked?"

"We've sent three different updates to the captain," Jim said. "None of them made it to the public."

Pen leaned in to read the notes on the pad. "He's not going to send out everything on demand," she said. "When did this start?"

Jim pointed to three times. "Mostly today. He asked for updates, and this was all supposed to go out today."

"He might have more urgent things," Kalin said. He looked at Brianne, but she turned away. She shouldn't have let this get to the point that Andor and Jim worried. "Send Pen the details and she can ask someone to check to see if the captain received any of them."

"He did," Pen said. "Not to worry. There are a bunch of updates going out in the next little while. I suggested he leave the great news about the weapon until the end. Finish on a high note, right?"

Now Brianne looked back at him. "Good to know we haven't slipped off the radar."

"Do you mean the missing scouts?" Andor asked, holding out his own pad. "Is this true?"

ALL SCOUTS LOST flashed from the screen in large red letters.

Pen reached for the pad. "Who published this?"

Andor handed it to her and pointed to the ID link. "That Len guy. He says we can't trust the captain anymore. That he knew this hours ago."

The rest of the team crowded around now. Three more pads added to Andor's on the table; three different versions of the story.

"I need to go," Pen said. "This needs management." She ran for the door and disappeared in the direction of the captain's briefing room.

"Does it say how they got the news?" Kalin asked. He tried not to listen to the voice in his head telling him Brianne leaked the details.

"It's true then?" Wilma asked. "We're flying blind?"

"Did the enemy take them out?"

"Are we going to fight back?"

Kalin waved for everyone to stop. "We don't have a lot of details yet," he said. "The captain will announce soon. It was supposed to happen tomorrow, but I guess we can't wait now."

"The captain should have come clean. People won't trust him now," Brianne said.

The little accusing voice got louder. *If she didn't pass the information to Len, she should be as angry as me.*

"Whoever leaked the information just caused a lot of panic for nothing," Kalin said. "We don't know what happened other than the fact they went dark."

"People have a right to be kept informed," Brianne said. "If the captain had been honest, no one would need to leak the information."

"I have to get to my family," Jim said. "My brother-in-law is a scout."

"Be careful," Kalin said. "It might be a bit rough outside."

The other team members slipped out within minutes of Jim leaving. Kalin and Brianne were alone. He sat at the table and flicked open his pad. The same message. And one from the captain to report. "Did you receive this?"

Brianne looked at her own pad and nodded. "I guess we're in trouble."

"Why? I didn't leak the information," Kalin said. "Did you?"

"Why would I do that?"

"You said you lost confidence in the captain. You did nothing to calm them down. Are you trying to make him look like a fool?"

She smiled. "I didn't say I'd lost confidence. I said people are going to lose it. Leaking the information wouldn't help me out. Anyway, there were so many people who knew, word was bound to get out."

"And there are plenty of people in the fleet who are happy to be the troublemakers." He pointed to his screen again. "This doesn't give any facts, and it doesn't offer anything but fear. What the hell are we supposed to do either way?"

"Not for us to decide. We should go to the captain before he orders us again." Brianne picked up her pad and headed to the door.

Kalin followed, trying to think of some kind of solution the fleet could live with and not blindly waste their only weapon. At least the message didn't mention its existence — yet.

34

———

Kalin leaned back and closed his eyes. It had been a night of futile guessing and tracking down the leak. The captain had ordered him, Pen, and Asher to try to locate the person, but there were too many possibilities. Now he was sitting in the captain's briefing room with Pen, waiting to talk about the communication, his relief at Brianne's absence tainted with worry that she was a suspect.

The captain entered alone. That didn't bode well for them. The only reason Kalin could think of that the civilian leader wasn't in the room was that they were about to be reprimanded.

He and Pen both stood at attention. *She must think the same.*

"At ease," the captain said. He waved them to sit as he did the same. "I need your input on the situation. The fleet has increased speed to the maximum. We don't have time to evacuate another ship. The planet will be in sight within forty-eight hours. How long before we absolutely need to do a fleet-wide communication?"

"If I may ask," Kalin said. The captain nodded for him to go ahead. "Why are we waiting to tell people?"

"Before I answer, what did you see out there when you searched for the source?"

"Lots of muttering and unrest," Pen said. "We couldn't get in too close because people would recognize us even in our hoods and casuals. Asher kept us from being noticed."

"Any outright rebellion?" Kalin asked.

The captain was trying to make them figure out the answer. Kalin mulled over the events. Like Pen said, muttering about secrets. Some threats to act, but nothing overt. People arguing that they should let the leaders run the ship like they had for generations. "You are already trying to keep the reaction down," he said. "Right now, it's only rumor. The scouts could be offline on purpose to avoid tracking. Do you know where Len is? How many people he's got with him?"

"He's being detained for his own protection." The captain didn't say anything more, so Kalin kept thinking. If the leadership was waiting with a purpose, why?

"Because once you announce, it becomes real," Pen said. She sat up. "Why didn't I think of that before?"

"Asher knew," Kalin said. "That's why he kept steering us away."

"Exactly," the captain said. "You didn't think of it, Pen, because your job is to communicate, and you Kalin because you are still getting used to our ways."

"The announcement still needs to go out," Pen said. "We can't wait until we are on Damu. We need unity. You need their trust."

"It is possible that we aren't facing mutiny because we are in space," the captain said. "But with only two days, we need to shift our thinking. We need leaders who think beyond the immediate but can also react quickly to threats when we land."

"Us?" Pen asked. "I'm not ready for that."

"No one is," the captain said. "But yes. You and Kalin, and Jo, if he's survived. Young people, adaptable people. Roger Whitnal and his peers are engaged in the same process as we speak."

"Any idea who he's recruiting?" Kalin asked.

"I gave him permission to speak to any of the military people he chose. It seemed only fair since I took Asher Jones." He stood and paced the room. "This is not to be announced, understand? You will begin to act as the leaders, but people must first accept your actions."

"Yes, sir." Kalin pushed aside his ideas of settling for a simple job on Damu. If the captain thought he was ready to lead, he would try. "But the scouts. We do need to tell people what we know, and about the weapon. They need hope to help them through the next couple of days."

"We should do it this evening," Pen said. "As soon as they hear, you'll need support. Everyone will have questions."

"One of the reasons we've waited. Certain plans needed to be set in motion before Roger and I become in demand. If we do it tonight, we can use the preparations for landing as an excuse to avoid questions."

Kalin started planning how to disband his team completely to avoid discussing the announcement. Then he stopped. He should be there for them to mitigate Brianne's influence. And if he was honest with himself, he was trying to avoid her — not a leadership quality.

"I think you might also want to tell them what you've been doing since the scouts went silent," he said.

"Will that make it easier on them?"

Not a question really. The captain didn't want the answer, but he was testing them again, or maybe only him. "No. But it will show you care. That you've been trying to locate them. Sending drones. Making plans to protect everyone. Finding a way to get us to Damu sooner."

"What about the protest leaders?" Pen asked. "Just because the most vocal one is under control, doesn't mean it's over."

The captain smiled. "I expect a tactic to avoid that very action to be in my script, Pen." He stood and checked his pad. "I have another meeting. I expect a draft in an hour."

As soon as they were alone, Kalin took in a deep breath. He had no clue that Asher was manipulating them last night. He couldn't be sure if it was his own naivety, or Asher's skill. But if he was going to lead the colony, he needed to stop believing people had only one agenda.

"I wonder when Asher learned this." Pen was typing as she spoke. "And I wonder how much loyalty he owes the captain."

Pen's distrust of Asher confused Kalin. He came across like a friend, but she always made some comment about him. Yes, he was a spy. And yes, he might have tortured Kalin if ordered, but those actions weren't personal, just jobs he did. And the man had saved her life.

"It is possible that his loyalty to Whitnal or the captain isn't important. What about his loyalty to you and Jo? And me, I guess."

She stopped typing and looked at him. "What? Why would that matter?"

He felt a rush of pride. He'd seen something Pen missed. "I mean, I don't think the captain, and maybe Whitnal, plan to lead the colony for more than the settling in phase. They are looking for the next generation, right?"

She chewed her lip while she thought about it. "I can't be sure. We've always talked about elections. A transition for a while, then people vote."

"And you don't think they are setting us up to be the ones people elect?"

She turned back to her pad. "I hope not. Not what I planned at all."

35

People of all ranks filled the observation room, and Brianne struggled to keep her small team separate from Kalin's. Their own working room would be better for this, but they had been ordered here. Perhaps to be recognized for creating the weapon, if Pen had bothered to put that in the communication.

In private it would be easier to say what she wanted and find out what she suspected: that Kalin knew something she didn't.

More people pushed into the room and Brianne found herself shoved closer to Kalin. If she couldn't just observe, she could ask questions. "Should we call security?" She kept her voice low.

He turned to her and then looked around. "People seem curious, not restless. The captain knows what he's doing."

"He's taken long enough to tell people what's going on," she said. Movement next to her caught her attention. The team surrounded them, affording a buffer zone whether they intended to or not. She was in the center of a small circle with Kalin and Pen. Good or bad, she could talk more freely. "I would have done it a day ago. And I would have protected my people."

"You need to stop thinking about yourself," Kalin said. "Everyone in the fleet is 'our people,' and maybe there's a bigger story you don't know about."

She stared at the screens for a moment, trying to bring her anger under control. He shouldn't talk to her that way. It wasn't her fault that she'd been kept in the dark.

"Did someone tell you about this bigger picture?" she asked when she could control her emotions.

"No," Kalin said.

"Are you happy to be here?" she asked again. Maybe he finally reacted to her because he was afraid, too. Afraid of a fight in tight quarters. Afraid of being blamed.

"This is where the captain wants us." He took a half step away, getting closer to Pen.

Maybe she could get something from the person who wrote the communication. Brianne leaned around him. "What about you, Pen? You must have more details than us lowly lieutenants."

"You need to wait like everyone else," Pen whispered. "Trust that the captain and the other leaders know what they are doing."

In other words, I'm not telling you anything.

The buffer around them was shrinking. More people squeezing in to learn the facts. The broadcast was going out to all the public screens, but not the individual ones. No one got the chance to hide in their room and brood. A good tactic as long as the security team stood poised to quell a revolt.

"Why can't he just get on with it?"

The crowd was close enough for Brianne to make out the muttered comments.

"We all know the truth anyway," a woman said. "My boy is a scout. He wouldn't leave me worried."

"Time to pick ourselves a better leader."

"Hear him out," a man said. "If we don't like what he says, we don't need to wait for Damu to make a change."

Brianne looked toward the door. If she was right about the reaction, she needed to leave as soon as the announcement ended. Between her and the exit was a sea of faces. All turned toward the screens. She touched her hip before remembering they'd been ordered to leave weapons locked up.

The screens flickered. Then the captain and Whitnal appeared. Behind them on screens stood the other captains and civilian leaders. A handful of the protest leaders with them.

"Thank you for coming together," the captain said. He introduced the people on the screens, who were talking to their own audiences by the way they pointed, introducing everyone to their ship's complement. The protest leaders nodded and then stared at the cameras. A sign of solidarity? Of capitulation?

"Let me start by addressing the rumors about the scouts. Yes, we have lost contact with them and the drones we sent out to find them. Let me be very clear. There is no evidence of their fate. If they live, they will join us on Damu, or before. If the worst happened, we will honor them as heroes."

He paused as though knowing people would need a moment to digest the information. Knowing the rumors were probably true and hearing the facts were two completely different things.

Brianne heard a sob and a quiet plea to the universe for her son escape the woman who'd spoken earlier.

No voices raised in anger. No one said anything. She looked around again to gauge her need to exit. Every face turned to the screen, waiting for the next awful announcement.

"We have no evidence that the enemy ship is pursuing us, or that they were responsible for whatever happened to the scouts. We are going to act as though they are. We will arrive on Damu in the next day. Our evacuation plan is laid out. You will receive the details on your pads, and your personal roles will be highlighted.

"A weapon is on the planet, ready to be used. One that will protect us in the event of an attack. We plan to do everything we can to avoid a battle. Every person in the fleet is valuable. Every person in the fleet has a role in our future.

"I ask you to act on your instructions and save your grief until we are safe. I know that is hard and I hope, along with you, that our scouts will return. That our children, brothers, sisters, and friends are safe and on their way."

He saluted the crowd and then the screen went back to showing the space and stars everyone knew from years of familiarity.

Brianne felt the buzz of her pad. Her instructions. Others in the crowd reached for their own devices. The muttering started again, and Brianne braced for the fight.

"I'm assigned to the packing group," the woman said. All traces of anger and pain gone. "If I have time after that, the shuttle bay."

The crowd started dispersing; people talked about their next tasks as they left.

"I'll see you before we head down," Pen said. She gave Kalin a kiss on the cheek and ran out reading her pad.

"I'm on the decoy group," Kalin said. "You?"

He didn't even look at his pad. Kalin had already known what it would say.

Brianne pulled hers out, trying to seem like she was just checking something she'd been told before. "Yeah. I'm on the data team."

"Good thing we all have an hour to pack our personal stuff," he said. "Plenty of time, though I guess the civilians might feel rushed. I'll see you on the ground unless our assignments change."

She nodded and watched him slide through the crowd. There was no time to change what happened. Data transfer might be a boring job, and it gave her no chance to talk to anyone about her role, but it did give her time to figure out what her future looked like on Damu.

36

K alin waved at Pen through the shelter window as she boarded her shuttle for the planet. He stood with Whitnal and the captain as the shuttles departed. Only one would remain, the smallest. Six people were headed for the decoy point, each with some supplies and any last-minute items they could find to take off the ship before it blew up. On the other nine ships, teams of three waited the same way. Only *Dark Prospect* was willing to risk the two leaders. By the time the assignment was over, the colonists would at least be sheltered and searching for food. The rations on the remaining shuttles would only last the few days they needed to travel back to the planet.

The outer bay doors closed, and the blast doors lifted. They were alone.

"It won't be long," Whitnal said. "I promised my constituents I would be back within two days."

"Did they believe you?" Kalin asked. "I mean, you can't guarantee everything will go right."

"I couldn't just leave," Whitnal said. "They are aware we're headed out to destroy the fleet ships. They believe that the enemy will be fooled. They also know the weapon is on Damu."

Hope is probably useful.

"It's worth the risk of death to avoid the set-up work," the captain said. "It will be chaos. Better that the other captains take the blame for every petty complaint."

Kalin laughed. "And we can come in and sort out any problems when we return."

The captain slapped him on the back. "Thinking like a politician. I really don't care if it goes well, and no one needs me. I am looking forward to retiring and leaving the problems to younger minds."

"I'll be happy to take you on as a consultant," Whitnal said. "I plan on a long career leading the first colony."

Since no ships would ever dock here again, they wandered the whole shuttle bay. Kalin checked the screens listing the progress. "Three shuttles are returning." That was not the plan. Was the planet unsuitable? Were they about to undo all the hard work and head out into space again?

"I wish we had better comms," Whitnal said.

"We agreed to dismantle the comms. We don't want to leave a sign that we are here," the captain said. "Tracking the progress is passive and safe. Are they coming here? Are there any more?"

"No sign of mass return," Kalin said. "But the only live feeds are for our shuttles."

"Let's not assume a problem," Whitnal said. "In fact, I'm curious about the progress. Nice not to need to wait until we get back."

Two minutes later the bay alarm started and Kalin led the way to the shelter. The doors would open when the shelter door sealed. If the shuttles flew close together, they'd know within ten minutes what was happening. Kalin checked his weapon. If the shuttles were full of anyone other than their own pilots, he'd take a few with him to death.

The three shuttles entered as soon as the doors were wide enough. Tight formation like that was banned in normal circumstances, but he wasn't sure he would have been able to resist the urge to show off a bit with the same opportunity.

"Report," the captain said as he strode through the shelter door the moment it was safe.

The three shuttle pilots grinned and lined up at attention. The first one began, "The planet is perfect. As much as we have seen, anyway. We're back because there's room to offload more supplies. Shuttles are going back to all ships."

"What supplies?" Whitnal said. "Did you bring someone to help load? I'm afraid only one of us is fit enough."

The pilot lifted his chin to the walled off section of the bay. "No need. We figured it might be a possibility. The mechs can load the prepared pallets fast and we can head out."

More food would be good, but it was a risk. "Who gave the order?" Kalin asked.

"The committee did the prep," the pilot said. His buddies headed for the pallets. "Pen gave the okay, but a bunch of people came to the decision."

"Things are working then," Whitnal said. "How was the landing?"

"Smooth. A couple of bruises and broken bones from overcrowding, but nothing serious. Skies are clear and we'll be off ship in ten. You can depart on schedule."

It was interesting to see how the pilot seemed comfortable talking casually. The military would need a strong reminder of proper respect. Kalin thought the captain needed to be down on the planet, but the decision was made, and he wouldn't push. At least Pen was part of the team wielding authority. She'd stop them going too far before they returned.

"Will you take all the extra supplies down in one trip?" the captain asked. "We plan to leave as soon as space is clear. I don't want to be dodging shuttles."

"The operation is coordinated to the second," the pilot said. "One trip. Fifteen minutes and out. We won't get in the way, sir."

"Very well," the captain said. "Looks like you'll be ahead of schedule."

Kalin turned to where the captain pointed. Six mechs guided pallets toward the shuttles. The other two pilots waited to secure the loads.

"If you'll excuse me," the pilot said. He saluted and ran to his shuttle.

"I hope we're not in for any more surprises," Whitnal said. "So, the countdown starts in thirty minutes."

The ships were leaving on a staggered schedule. Without comms, they had to trust the other ships would do as planned. *Dark Prospect* was the last on the list. In just over an hour, the captain would authorize the autonav to head for the planet where they would blow up the fleet. A day away from Damu. Not far enough for Kalin to feel secure, but enough. The shuttles contained plenty of power to return.

"What are you planning to do for the next day?" Whitnal asked. "The last we'll spend on board."

"Sleep?" Kalin said. "And maybe get through a lot of the remaining rations."

"Shuttle simulations," the captain said, "and sleep. I think it will be in short supply for a while. You, Roger?"

"I'll wander the ship. I need to say goodbye. And then sleep," he laughed. "Perhaps we should schedule a final dinner tonight. Give us time to heal from a hangover before we are forced to endure our own overcrowding."

There was no reason to be alert during the trip, Kalin thought. "I guess I'll do some simulations, too. I'm not sure I can sleep that long."

"Then we should meet in my quarters at nineteen hundred," the captain said. "Kalin, you are in charge of food. I'll ensure we have plenty to drink."

The shuttle alarm started blaring again.

37

Kalin pushed Whitnal toward the shelter and grabbed for his own weapon. The captain did the same and they backed in through the shelter. Inside, they watched the bay doors open. If this was an attack, they were trapped. The weapon in his hand wouldn't shoot through the window or the walls. Being inside only stopped them from being dragged into vacuum as the atmosphere vented. But holding the matte gray stun gun made Kalin feel like he was doing something.

When the doors opened halfway, a ship slipped in and landed at the far end of the bay. A second later, another ship cleared the space. A third followed and then the doors began to lower. Someone on one of those ships had the access codes.

Someone on one of the three scout ships that now stood in the bay waiting for their flight drive to cycle down.

The seconds dragged by for Kalin. The bay doors needed to fully close before the shelter would open. How long would it take for the scout ships to shut down? He leaned against the glass staring at the first ship, afraid to hope one of their missing crew waited inside. Terrified to think it was the start of an alien attack. Not ready to experience the other side of an invasion.

The captain and Whitnal stood close, each focused on a ship.

"We should have had suits in here," Whitnal said. "I'd rather be out there in the bay with room to move."

"If we could get out, you'd be flailing around in zero gravity. Be patient," the captain said.

Whitnal stepped away from the window and the spell broke. It was not realistic to think the enemy had captured the scouts. They destroyed what they found and moved on.

The bay doors finally closed and the lock on the shelter clicked to tell them the bay was safe. The alarm settled down. Kalin moved to be the first out, but the captain held him back before stepping through.

Three mechanical sighs filled the bay. The pilot door to each scout ship hinged open. The first one out was Jo.

Kalin holstered his weapon and ran to hug his friend. "Pen is going to be very happy."

"Where is everyone?" Jo said. "I was expecting a bit of congestion in here."

"Already on Damu," the captain said. "You will join them as soon as you've reported and refueled."

The other two scouts were waiting behind Jo. The woman spoke, "We can refuel. Jo knows everything." She looked around. "Is there fuel on Damu? We should take as much as we can."

Kalin didn't think the shuttles had left anything behind that was vital for their settlement. Yes, there were machines and panels of material to manufacture basics, but they were manual or solar-powered. "You should fill your auxiliary tanks. You won't be going far."

At a nod from the captain, the two pilots ran to activate the refuel processes. Mechs rumbled out of niches in the walls of the bay. Kalin wondered if this was happening on any other ship. Or if the departure schedule was on track.

"This is it," Jo said as though reading his mind. "The enemy took out the others. Our position in the back of the formation saved us. Everything happened fast, but we spun away at the first attack." He closed his eyes, the emotions leaking out as he tried to gain control. "We don't think anything followed us. Our sensors didn't pick up a ship anyway. I think..."

When Jo didn't continue, Kalin touched his arm. "You did the right thing. You couldn't save them, and we needed to know."

Jo looked at him and Kalin found kinship in his eyes. They had both lost friends in battle. It never felt right. No matter how tragic the loss seemed, their job was to protect people. To take risks. To put themselves in harm's way for others. Knowing that could mean death didn't make the reality any easier to live with.

"What were you going to say?" the captain asked.

Jo blinked. "I think they knew our destination. Maybe not the exact location, but close enough. And maybe the scouts they destroyed just hit a shield. That it wasn't an active attack, but a defense."

"Because if they were attacking, you wouldn't have escaped?" the captain asked.

Jo shrugged. "I guess so. But we didn't see any weapons or fighters."

"Working on guesses is getting harder as we go deeper," Whitnal said. "Well, the weapon is on Damu. Our plan is still the best we can come up with. We should stick to the schedule."

"The plan, sir?" Jo asked.

"The first ships have started their journey to the decoy point. We are scheduled to leave soon. We'll destroy the fleet in one location, come back on the shuttles, hoping we fool the enemy. Plan to use the weapon if they see through the ruse, even if it means we are destroyed on approach."

"We'll be happy to escort you," Jo said. "Even three scouts could make the difference."

"You head to the planet," the captain said. "People down there are waiting for you. Tell them what happened."

"And a lot of them will be heartbroken because it's only the three of us," Jo said. "Are you sure you don't need us?"

"We're consolidating into five shuttles. A risk, yes, but the fewer we are, the less likelihood we'll be found."

The woman strode up and saluted. "Fueling complete and awaiting orders."

"Go to Damu," Whitnal said. "We will be leaving by the time you are halfway there."

The three pilots stood for a few more seconds, rigid at attention, like they struggled for something. As if considering offering to join them one more time, a discipline breach, but the rules were changing and perhaps it was time to do what they thought right, not simply follow orders. Then their bodies relaxed, and they nodded before marching off to their ships. Kalin noticed a few cartons being shoved behind the seats.

The alarm sounded and Kalin led the other two to the shelter. This would be the last time they needed the protection. The next time the bay doors opened would be for the shuttle back to Damu.

"I don't envy them," Whitnal said. "It is wonderful that

they survived, but their appearance will signal the loss of so many more."

"If everything works, they will be the last to fall to a battle," the captain said.

Not quite true, Kalin thought. Settling the planet would cost lives.

38

W hen they'd landed, Brianne was surprised to see how welcoming the planet was. She stood with the others in one of the two grassy clearings close to each other; perfect for the mass landing as if designed for the purpose. Trees surrounded the clearings, tall and high-canopied, giving natural protective cover. The air almost sweet. No sign of large animals, but a few flocks of birds settled in after the commotion of the arrival was done.

Now, two days later, Brianne was finally getting somewhere. Without Kalin to interfere, it was easy to convince the other ship leaders that she was indispensable. She knew what to do with the weapon, and that was vital now. The rest of the colonists, assigned jobs like creating shelter and testing local flora and fauna for suitable food, would be easy to lead.

Now, Kalin was back. The ships sat at the decoy point, timers counting down to destruction. The weapon sat mounted on its track and pointed skyward.

All captains assembled in the tent along with the civilian leaders. Kalin, Jo, and Pen in the middle of the group. Asher stood next to the captain and Brianne on the outside. No one had told her to leave yet, and she intended to keep silent so they wouldn't. If they told her to leave, she knew it would mean they didn't support her. And she would just be one of the herd when the time came to pick the new power structure. She'd spent too much time building credibility in this group to let it go.

"The population is situated mainly by ship of origin. The wooded areas proved safe, so shelters are scattered throughout. Unless the enemy can scan for lifeforms through the dense canopy, we are safe for now." Della, the woman who'd been the civilian leader on *The Orchard*, was finishing the update to the newcomers.

"The ships should be destroyed in two hours," Whitnal said. "The operation went without flaw, and we found a few items that might be useful."

"How long before we decide conditions are safe enough for us to disperse?" another civilian leader asked. "This area won't support us for long. And we need to start the livestock clones growing and get food stuff manufacturing up and running."

"That's the question," Captain Odsmundsen said. She had to stop thinking of him as the captain, and her captain seemed too weird. Too many others held that title, and for the first time more than one captain was in attendance. "Jo, how far can the scouts range? We need all the details so we can finalize the plan."

What plan? Maybe I should have volunteered to go with the ships. Something big happened.

"We can do a few orbits before the fuel is gone," Jo said. "The ships are in good repair, but we have no way of keeping them that way."

"How far out do you think the enemy is?" Whitnal asked.

"Their ship is on the way?" Della asked. "When did we learn that?"

Brianne smiled. At least she wasn't the only one kept in the dark. She could use that to her advantage.

"I asked the scouts to keep that detail under wraps," Odsmundsen said. "We didn't need panic infecting your work when you couldn't do anything about it. But we were able to benefit from the information." He included everyone in the tent from the decoy mission in that 'we.'

"And?" Della didn't seem angry to be left out. This was a power play, and she would recognize the tactic, so she wasn't actually oblivious. Brianne watched her carefully to learn how not to lash out. "What's the big discovery?"

"We found a second Z-converter," Kalin said at a nod from Odsmundsen. "We can test the weapon."

The tent went silent. Brianne held her breath. Testing didn't mean they'd be confident of the outcome, but it would feel like one less layer of uncertainty.

"How quickly can you arrange this test?" Della asked.

"First, I think we should keep the general population uninformed," Whitnal said. "We need to tell them everything at once. The test results, the presence of the enemy, any plans we can formulate after the test."

"Plans to attack?" The words fell out before Brianne thought. Damn, she was supposed to observe. Now they can tell her to go.

"We have no way of attacking," Kalin said. "The shuttle is grounded as the weapon mount. The scouts have enough fuel to witness the test, and maybe that will be all they can do. The weapon won't fit in a scout ship. We need plans to survive."

How dare he berate me?

"If we can use the weapon twice, we should keep it for attacking. A test is a waste," she said, trying to turn her earlier statement into more of a suggestion. She was in no position to order people — yet.

Asher whispered something to the captain and then said, "Brianne, we worried all along that the weapon won't even work. If we conduct a test, even if the results just confirm the range it's capable of, we'll be better off."

There was no coming back from that. Brianne nodded and waited for the discussion to continue. No matter how hard it was, she'd find another way to win.

"We think the best approach is to aim the weapon toward a known point, and then discharge it, as soon as we can, so we have time to make adjustments," one of the other captains said.

Brianne hadn't bothered to remember the names of the minor players. It was clear her captain and Whitnal held the power.

"Now we can send the scouts," Jo said. "We can range for the enemy and find a place to plant a target."

"The shuttles you brought back," Della said. "You plan to blow them up?"

Whitnal tossed a pad on the table. "We had time to do a few calculations. If we transfer most of the fuel to one shuttle, it should be enough to park it somewhere. The scouts can point us to a location. The autonav can drive the thing in place. We test if the weapon can find the shuttle, then we fire."

"The scouts should be out of the way," Pen said. "Far enough that they won't get caught up, but close enough to see the results."

"One scout," Jo said. "I'll do that. The other two can keep looking for the enemy until they need to return for good."

Everything was moving fast, and no one was asking for her input. Brianne listened with only half her attention. She looked around the room. Only two people who could fire the weapon: Kalin and her. Anyone else who might know because they were involved in the design or build were out assembling shelters or testing local plants and animals for food sources.

"I'll attend the weapon," she said. "I know how it is supposed to work."

"Thank you," Odsmundsen said. "We need Kalin on comms to make the final adjustments."

The comms had proved a bit unreliable since they landed, but at least they had some.

"You'll need someone with you," Whitnal said. "Jo will be in orbit, Kalin in here with us."

"I can do it alone," she said. Having anyone watching would restrict her ability to tweak the test to her advantage. And this might be her last chance.

"Pen," Della said, "if you don't have anything more pressing, Brianne will need a runner at least."

39

Three days on Damu and Kalin was starting to believe the enemy had moved on to another target. But without proof, no one could afford to relax. The scouts were settling in at a distance from the shuttle, which was parked as far as they dared to move away from the planet. After a lot of discussion about the makeup of the groups, Brianne, Pen and Della joined him, waiting to initiate the test. Brianne's insistence she could do it alone had been ignored.

The other leaders listened to the comms. One of the many inconveniences of planet life, there was no way to spread the technology around to where the colonists might need it. Pen would hustle back to the others as soon as he pressed the button. The other two would stay with him to assess any effect on the weapon.

"How does this work again?" Della asked. "I don't mean the test. Yes, we have the coordinates and can aim for the target. But when we need the weapon for the enemy, how will we aim? The scouts are going to be grounded from lack of fuel soon."

If they could just make it through the test, Kalin thought. All the answers were available, but this test needed to be completed. "We'll conserve the fuel," Kalin said. "After this, we need the scouts to give us notice of the enemy's approach."

"I'm sorry," Della said. "I'm nervous. I keep wondering how we'll survive if the test fails."

He wanted to tell her that worrying about something they would know in a few minutes was a useless waste of energy, but he felt the same anxiety. Too many unknowns, and every answer contained another question.

"Why are we waiting?" Brianne asked. "We have the coordinates. The scouts are set to observe. We should fire and get it over with."

Kalin stood beside the ignition button. Brianne knew the answer to that question. They had agreed on the timing. With uncertain comms, they couldn't do anything but stick to the plan. She moved closer and he stood to block her access. This was his job, not hers.

He wished Brianne could be the runner so he could talk to Pen after. All they would be sure of is that the weapon fired — or didn't. But Brianne had knowledge about the specs, so she would help with the assessment while they waited. Della had the authority to make decisions. Pen took the responsibility of communications.

"It will be good to know," Della said. "Either way, people need to be made aware of what's happening. They are stuck right now regardless of the outcome today."

Brianne walked around the weapon, checking the attachments for the tenth time. Kalin kept her in sight. He couldn't get over the feeling that she planned to do something that they couldn't reverse. Paranoia, maybe, but recognizing it as such didn't help settle his nerves. He tried to tell himself that she wouldn't sabotage their only chance at winning a war — on purpose at least. She still wanted recognition, but not that kind. Unfortunately, damaging the weapon by accident would be as devastating as an actual attack.

"One minute," Pen said. "Brianne, join us, please."

Brianne looked up from where she was poking at the welds holding the weapon to the rails on the shuttle floor. "Just a final look," she said.

"Now," Della said.

The tone didn't leave room for argument. Brianne stood and glared at Kalin. Then she strode over to join the other two in the pilot section.

"Thirty seconds," Pen said.

The shuttle should disintegrate when hit with the pulse. When he pressed the button, it would be a few minutes before the scouts would see the result. By the time Pen reached the command tent, they would know.

The scouts were to return to Damu as soon as they reported. If comms dropped, it would be an hour or more before they had an answer. And if the weapon missed, would it be a beacon for the enemy to find them?

"Time," Pen said.

Kalin hit the ignition button.

The weapon whined and then vibrated. No sign of it working beyond that. No beam of light penetrating the atmosphere. The absence of explosions allowed them to keep the test a secret, but a sign might have lowered the stress burning through his veins.

Pen moved to his side. "It worked. I'm sure we'll be okay. Gotta go." She sprinted past the weapon and headed toward the command tent.

"Kalin, get back here," Brianne said as she walked

around to check the braces again. "We have work to do. You can daydream later."

He ran his hand along the casing. No heat, no cracks, dents, or burst seams. "It's like nothing happened," he said.

Della paced around the shuttle. "Let's hope that's not a sign. What else are you checking?"

"The braces held," Brianne said. "Although the thing hardly moved, so no surprise. Kalin, change places."

The inspection plan had them double checking each other's work. Kalin looked over the panel one more time before letting Brianne take over.

Nothing was obviously wrong.

"You ready to open the casing up?" Brianne asked. "See if the insides survived?"

They were certain the Z-converter would burn out. What they didn't know was if that would damage the circuits. Everything was as shielded as possible, and they had replacements for all the important parts, but repairs would take time. The weapon would be offline for as long as it took.

Brianne didn't ask again. She flipped the hinges and lifted the lid.

No smell of burning wires. Kalin relaxed.

"Well?" Della asked.

He held his hand over the converter shielding. Not hot. Was he expecting it to be?

"I think it's safe," he said.

Brianne unscrewed the bolts and lifted the cover. "Looks fine," she said.

"Pull it for testing," Della said. "If the Z-converter survived, does that mean we can fire the weapon more than once?"

They had been so sure something critical would fail,

Kalin couldn't dig up the details of the rest of the components.

"Not forever," Brianne said. "But some components we can manufacture when the factories are up and running. But that will be too late. We have no idea how long it will take to reload, so to speak, and we won't know until it fails how long we can use the weapon."

Kalin placed the Z-converter in a crate. "We need the techs in here."

"When we are sure the test worked," Della said.

"It did," Pen yelled as she raced into the shuttle. "The thing disintegrated. Lock up and come back to command. Time to celebrate."

One thing, Kalin thought. Only one little step forward.

40

The weapon was ready. The relief from that test had carried Kalin for a few minutes, then the work reminded him there were so many more problems to solve.

Now, after a day of argument over tiny details and suppositions, the new Z-converter was in place even though the old one seemed to be fine. The techs decided it was too big a risk that the old one would fail mid-fire. Now they waited. The scouts were on their final run as a team to search the area around Damu for signs of the enemy. After this, only one scout would go, and soon after that, they would be out of fuel. Then the business of settling the planet would be priority number one.

Kalin, Pen, and Brianne huddled with the leaders working to identify the first steps of filling the local area with farms and homes while they waited for news.

"We need more than just these plans," Whitnal said. "We need someone to go exploring. This landing area isn't big enough to support us for anything more than a few months."

Kalin tuned out the conversation. Brianne was in the middle of it, making sure she knew what the choicest assignments were and generally sucking up to everyone who might help her become important. He didn't want to put any more energy into keeping her from screwing things up. They were on the planet, and she couldn't do much damage now.

"I'd like to do that exploring," Pen said, handing him a cup of tea. "When we aren't worried about the attack. I don't know if I can settle into a farm or some kind of manufacturing. And I don't want a leadership role."

"What about Jo?" Kalin asked. "Do you see us exploring together? Three intrepid adventurers?"

She burst out laughing and gained a few looks from the group huddled over the survey map. "I don't know what he's planning, but I was thinking you and me alone."

"It's weird," Kalin said. "We've been a group for so long and now we get to make our own decisions about the future. And I don't care what the captain wanted; I am not taking on the leadership either. I guess it's time to start thinking beyond following orders."

"Asher is going to work with the government, whoever that turns out to be. He said he wasn't interested in being the face of the leadership either, more fun in leading from behind."

So, no change. Would the colony break down into the same groups as the ships? "We should think of ourselves as one now. No more my ship or your ship. We are all here."

"I agree. I think it will take a while to get there, though," Pen said.

The comms crackled. "Plan A. Plan A. Plan A." It sounded like Jo, but the comm shut down before any more came through.

Kalin heard the whine of the scout ship engines pass overhead. Someone would give the full report soon, but they couldn't wait.

"We need people to move farther under cover," Captain Odsmundsen said. "Kalin, Pen, as soon as we have the details, head for the weapon."

The enemy was on its way. Plan A was to hide and prepare for attack.

Brianne muttered something to Whitnal and slipped out of the tent. She must be heading for the bulk of the colony. No matter the details of the report, they had to make sure humanity was safe.

Jo entered the tent at a run. "Five ships. Definitely headed here."

Five?

We only have one weapon, one shot, then it takes too much time to prepare for a second. There is no way we can manage to take out five ships.

Kalin noticed Brianne slip back into the tent. Too soon for her to have made it to the camp and back.

"Coordinates?" Captain Odsmundsen asked. "Any estimate on lead time?"

"Clustered," Jo said. He rattled off the location and then grabbed a container of water. "They were moving slowly. I can't be sure they still are."

"We can't send you back," the captain said. "We can make it hard for them to find us though. The camp will retreat deeper into cover. We can camouflage this tent more. The weapon?"

"We can adjust the aim for that area of space," Kalin said, checking the coordinates again.

"We should aim and shoot now," Brianne said. "Get them before they can threaten the colony."

"We can't afford to miss," the captain said. "Adjust the aim and do your best to cover it. We need to be ready to fire when we acquire a target."

"Mr. Whitnal? Della?" Brianne said. "You and the other civilian leaders can't be okay with sitting here, waiting to be attacked."

Whitnal looked at her. Kalin thought he saw anger in his expression. "We will leave our defense to the military. Your captains and officers are much more capable of making decisions about fighting this threat."

Brianne deflated. She had no allies, and her last words probably destroyed her chance of gaining any. Kalin was surprised at the pity he felt.

"Of course," Brianne finally said. "I simply thought since we are on the planet, you would want a say."

"We need to get moving now," Pen said. "It will take hours to secure the camp properly. I'll go tell them to start."

"Thank you," the captain said. "As far from here as possible. They shouldn't take anything more than a few days' supplies."

Pen turned and ran for the camp.

"Where do we start?" Whitnal asked.

"Where are the scout ships?" the captain asked. "They need to be hidden, but ready to launch."

"I left the others doing that," Jo said. "We'll go and check the progress if you want."

"No." This was another captain. "Stay grounded for now. By my calculations, we'll see the enemy at the latest by tomorrow. If they are capable of more speed, it could be any minute."

The uncertainty was the biggest risk, Kalin thought. "People need tasks. Who is staying here?"

"The civilians should go with the camp," Brianne said. "If the military are in command, we need to be able to act."

"I'll stay as a representative," Whitnal said. "But she's right. No matter what happens, the camp will need guidance. If we all stay here, there's a chance we will all die."

The civilians grabbed water and ration bars and left with no argument.

"I think we need to minimize the number of people here regardless of position." The captain scanned the room. "Kalin, Joe, Pen, Brianne. You are the weapon team."

"One tech would be helpful," Kalin said, "and a few medics."

"It won't be a ground battle," the captain said, "but we should bring in a handful of soldiers just in case."

"I think we should all stay here until the situation changes." Whitnal ushered the last of the people to the entrance. "We are all capable of pulling camouflage over the tent and weapon."

The tent seemed empty with so few people inside. The weapon itself was a few minutes' run away. Soon this whole new life would either be started, or over.

41

W hen he let himself imagine what the appearance of the enemy would be like, Kalin never came up with the reality.

Five smallish ships hung in orbit. What were they waiting for? And why did they cluster like that? The weapon wasn't enough to take out all five, but they'd get two, maybe three ships seriously damaged with one well-placed shot.

"We should attack," Brianne said.

She'd been arguing the same point since the scouts discovered the ships. Now, a couple of hours had passed, and she couldn't be persuaded or ordered off the position.

"We can't sit here all day," the captain said. "I need more options. While they are stationary, we can work out the best move."

"Attacking is the only option," Brianne said.

Did she know how fear made her voice shrill?

"It's not," Kalin said. "Did you even read those battle records you found? You are assuming these are the ships that destroyed my people. What if they aren't? If we shoot first, we could be starting a war we have no hope of winning."

"We need them to reach out," Whitnal said. "If they are here for something other than the worst, we need to talk."

"I could take a scout," Jo said. "See if it causes a reaction."

"Not yet," Pen said. "You are our only option for leaving the planet."

"You'd run?" Brianne said, real shock showing on her face.

"No. They are scout ships," Pen said. "Only one person per ship. But if that's how you think..."

Kalin didn't want to listen to them fight. He'd take Pen's side. No, not her side, the right side. But if this was the last few hours they had, he wanted it to be violence-free. "We were discussing options," he said. "Is one of the ships fully fueled?"

Jo shook his head. "We hadn't gotten around to it. Mine will manage a fly-by. That leaves the others for anything you need to harry our visitors."

"They might not be aware we're here," Whitnal said. "We have no idea of their surveillance capabilities. If we stay put, they may leave. If we start running to ships and weapons, it may alert them to our presence."

"The population is going to stay under cover, but not forever," the captain said. "I won't either. But this moment is a gift. Any time we carve out to think about our actions is more valuable than a hundred weapons. Keep coming up with ideas."

Kalin didn't think they had any new approaches to offer. Attack or wait and see, what else could they do? "How about scanning for communications?"

"From the ship?" Whitnal asked. "You think they are reaching out and we're not listening?"

"No, or maybe. I know we need as much information as we can gather if we're going to help the captain make the best choice."

"Are there any records from before they arrived?" Pen asked. "It doesn't need to be them calling to us, maybe they are talking between ships."

The captain sent Brianne to look through the records and scan for differences in the ambient signals. It gave her something to do that didn't include constantly barking that they should attack.

"There's another thing I wondered," the captain said. "These ships all seem smaller than I expected. But what if they are one ship that can break down into multiple modules?"

Pen pulled out her pad, then looked around for a power source. "These are going to be useless soon," she muttered as she plugged into a port on the bank of servers. "Give me a minute. I think I captured some specs from the initial observations."

Now it was just the three of them. Whitnal, the man who seemed poised to become the leader of the colony, if they survived. The captain, who still led them until this threat no longer existed — and any new challenge the planet threw at them if they survived. And Kalin. He didn't belong here. He'd been part of the *Dark Prospect* team for only a few months. He barely understood the way they lived their lives on the ship. But perhaps he was the most qualified to help here on Damu. None of the other people on the planet had experienced the magnitude of change he had.

"Kalin." Whitnal's voice broke into his thoughts. "I'm

kind of surprised you aren't advocating for Brianne's idea of attacking first and thinking later."

Because that is exactly what they thought his people did. "There's no second chances if we do that."

"But you are a soldier, perhaps more than any of the military personnel on the planet."

"And I've killed more people than anyone here," he said. It hurt to be accused of this now. He'd let himself feel like his past was behind him. Not gone, but less valuable than all his actions since joining *Dark Prospect*.

"That's a low bar," Whitnal said. "I didn't mean that. I meant you have the most experience, and if you are advocating waiting, I think it's important for us to understand why."

He could still mean that I'm a killer. But maybe not. If I don't trust what he says, I'm no better than a mindless killer.

"If your ships had waited at the beginning of this whole journey to a new home, if they hadn't shot down my ships, would we have been adversaries?"

"It was a bad decision," Whitnal said, "but our philosophies were too different for us to be friends. No one really knows what it was like at the beginning. But I can guess it was highly charged and panicky. Bad conditions to make good choices in."

"He's not blaming us," the captain said, "any more than you were blaming him. He's right. If our ancestors had simply headed away from his, many more of us would be alive. Possibly we wouldn't be in this position now."

"I'm not sure we get the luxury of generations of hatred between us and this ship," Kalin said. "Maybe they need to be in space to do the damage they did to *The Righteous Storm*. Maybe being on Damu will make the difference. But if we attack first and they survive, we are dead."

"Okay," Whitnal said and then looked up from the plans. "It looks like Pen has something for us."

Pen looked up at her name. "Yeah. Still a guess, but the information supports that being the one ship we saw broken into modules. And I would guess they are self-sustainable. Otherwise, why bother?"

"There is some background signal that's too regular to be static," Brianne called from the comm stack. "I can't make anything out, but I'm pretty sure they are talking to each other and not us."

"Maybe they are having the same discussion up there," Pen said. "Maybe there is hope?"

The tent door opened, and three soldiers escorted a tech and a couple of medics. "Reporting for duty."

42

"What are you doing, Lieutenant Weaver?" the captain asked.

"We were under cover the whole way," the lead soldier said. "Don't worry. Thermal damping clothes, and we moved slow enough over the open ground to appear like a local fauna."

"You asked for them," Brianne said. She wasn't going to let herself be forgotten. No one seemed to want her idea, and she couldn't think of another one. All she knew was waiting wouldn't make them safe.

The captain acknowledged her comment and told the newcomers to set up. "We may need your clothes," he said. "At some point, we'll need to access our weapon."

Weaver let the others settle in the back of the tent after shedding their outer garments.

"Maybe we should get ready," Brianne said. "When we decide to fight, we need to do it fast."

"You won't want to spend a lot of time in those things," Weaver said. "Heavy and not exactly flexible."

"What's the mood in the camp?" Whitnal asked.

"Fear, patience, a bit of grumbling," Weaver said. "They want to know what we're going to do."

"Will they interfere?" Kalin asked. "Are we looking at a rebellion?"

Weaver grunted a laugh. "Not yet. Maybe not ever. They'll stay put for as long as they are afraid of those things." He pointed to the sky.

"It won't be long," the captain said. "I think we'll be looking at a day at most. If it isn't resolved by then, we'll need to get on with settling in."

"Eric, have you made a decision?" Whitnal asked. "The longer we take discussing the options, the fewer remain."

"We only have two real options," the captain said. "We strike first, or we wait and see. I think Kalin is correct in his assessment that striking first is the least desirable."

"Because we don't have enough firepower," Weaver said. "It's a good strategy — until it isn't."

"We only need a few minutes' notice," Kalin said. "If we had comms, I would be happy to wait at the weapon for orders, but we're blind. The ships are talking but not to us."

"You think they might try?" Weaver asked. "What will you say if they do start talking? If they start threatening or negotiating?"

Brianne pulled one of the thermal damping jackets off the pile and slipped it on. She kept one ear on the conversation while she made preparations.

"They don't seem like the type to threaten," the captain said. "They kill and move on. I'm hoping negotiation will come down to us agreeing to stay on the planet and let them do what they will in space."

"Do you think they are aware we're stuck?" Jo asked.

"Let's hope not," the captain said. "While we wait, we

should eat. If it comes to battle, we won't be able to take a dinner break."

Likely we won't be able to do anything ever again if we don't act.

Weaver hadn't been exaggerating. The jacket was like putting on a series of boards. Good thing she wouldn't need it in the shuttle because they were heavily shielded.

"How long?" Pen asked. "We can't wait forever. Like you said, at some point life just goes on."

"For now, that's in their hands," Whitnal said, nodding toward the ships above them. "I think we wait out a night at least."

Brianne stood near the entrance, watching. No one inside showed the tension she expected; too relaxed. Kalin opened a ration bar. Pen was pulling water containers together on the table. The soldiers and medics were chatting. It was like death didn't hang over their heads. Three of the people in this tent had been on a planet. They'd fought to survive and return to the safety of the ship, but they didn't grab for sidearms or camouflage. No one gave her orders. It was like they didn't remember she was there.

She was the only one who saw clearly. And she didn't do all that work to be here on the precipice of grabbing power to sit back and wait to die.

"If we have that long," Jo said, "maybe someone should be trying to set up the weapon for more shots. I mean, the first one didn't destroy the components. If we are able to fire enough, we might just wipe them out."

Finally, someone who agreed negotiation was useless. Brianne relaxed her stance and stepped away from the doorway.

"Five shots?" Kalin asked. "In quick succession, and re-aiming each time?"

"Even two would be better than one," Brianne said. "We test the speed of changing the Z-converter. If we adjusted the mounting, it's possible we can aim at a new point while it was happening."

"Would you be able to take them all out?" Weaver asked. "Once we attack, they will definitely shoot back. And we don't really know if one of the ships can do the damage we found. Maybe it needs all five, but maybe only one." He looked at her jacket but didn't say anything.

"There's no guarantees, Weaver," Brianne said. "One shot, five? It doesn't matter. Maybe they are waiting for more ships to show up, if more of them exist. Waiting won't change that."

"Nevertheless, we will wait." The captain didn't bother to look at her. His words came out curt and showed he was tired of the argument.

"Yes, sir," she said. No point in saying any more. She'd lost the fight. No one was on her side. There were too few people here to gather allies.

"Do we have the frequency of the ship comms?" Jo asked. "We could try to reach out to them. Give up on trying to pretend we're not here."

"If nothing comes by nightfall, we'll try that." The captain sat at the table. "What do we send? They are unlikely to understand any of our languages."

Brianne sidled closer to the exit.

"Math?" Weaver suggested. "It should be universal."

"To show them we are capable of higher thinking?" Pen said. "It might work. Unless higher thinking is a threat to them. I hate the not knowing stuff."

"No," Jo said. "You hate the not doing something stuff. You've jumped into plenty of situations without knowing everything."

Everyone chuckled. It sealed Brianne's feeling of isolation. Everyone understood the inside joke. Everyone except her. Pen was a wildcard. But for some reason everyone loved her. Well, if that's what it took, Brianne was done with waiting for permission. She slipped outside.

43

The hard part about waiting was the tension. Not able to relax enough to rest and with nothing to use up the nervous energy, Kalin watched the soldiers and medics talking quietly. The tech was working with Jo and Pen to see if there was any way to recharge the weapon faster. It would probably draw most of the power stored in batteries and the scout ships. But win or lose, the scouts were done. And the sooner the colony got used to being without a source of energy they couldn't replenish, the faster they'd set up the solar and wind devices.

Whitnal was sitting with the captain going over comms. If they could pull something out of the static, it would be worth the effort, but he was sure it was more to pass the time than any real hope.

Kalin looked around. "Anyone seen Brianne?" He didn't expect an answer. He knew where she was: with their weapon.

He saw the realization dawn on every face in the tent. He grabbed a camouflage jacket and his sidearm, then ran to the shuttle. There were only so many thermal damping units on the table. The captain could figure out who would get them.

It was quiet outside, as if everyone and everything on the planet was holding their breath, waiting for someone to start the battle. Looking up to their visitors, he didn't notice any change to their position. Still five ships. Still no indication of imminent attack.

He rounded the back end of the shuttle, keeping low to duck under the weapon. As he slipped inside, he heard the whine of the warming up cycle.

"Too late." Brianne depressed the ignition and then stood back arms in the air.

He spun and ran outside. Everyone except the medics raced toward him. The sky lit up and the ground shook. He looked up before thinking it was a bad idea. She'd destroyed four ships. How had she done that? No, wrong question. What were they going to do about the last ship? That was the priority.

The tech ran past. "I'll see what I can do," he said, "but don't expect miracles."

Kalin joined him inside, sidearm ready to stop Brianne if she tried anything. She stood backed up against the pilot seat, arms still up in surrender.

"How many?" she asked. No apology, no sign of regret.

"One left."

"Let's hope they need all five to kill us then."

"Are you insane?" Kalin strode toward her. "You killed us. We might not have had to fight. You took away our chance to try for a compromise. You've taken away any chance of peace."

"Step away, Kalin." Lieutenant Weaver nudged him to the side and reached for Brianne, restraints ready. "Congratulations. If we live, you'll be the first person to face colony justice."

Kalin fought the urge to show Brianne what that justice might be. He turned back to the group clustered around the weapon. "Any chance we can fire again? I don't care if we die doing it, we can't leave that ship just hanging in our space."

"The Z-converter blew," the tech said. "It's going to take hours to clean up the mess. There's enough power for one more, but we can't use the weapon until we repair it."

"So now we have to wait again," Whitnal said. "This time with no hope of acting."

"Take her out," the captain said. "We don't have a place to lock her up, so secure her to one of the trees."

"I can take a shuttle up," Jo said. "Maybe check for any activity around the ship."

"Not yet." The captain stepped away to give the tech room to work. "I'm not going to panic. The ship hasn't retaliated."

"It's moved out," Pen said as she slipped back inside. "Still there, still just waiting for something. I can see the ship, but I'm guessing Brianne gave them something to worry about."

"Perhaps one is not powerful enough," Whitnal said. "We've given it a shock."

"I don't like all the perhaps and maybes," the captain said. "Weaver, keep watch and report if anything changes. We can call up a few more techs from the colonists. I don't think hiding matters anymore."

Kalin agreed. Brianne had screwed them completely. Sure, she found a way to target four of five ships in one shot, but now they were at the mercy of that one ship. An enemy with a record of absolute destruction. One that hadn't tried to communicate. One that might not give any indication before whoever controlled the ship eliminated the threat. Perhaps the planet.

"I'll get you some help," the captain said to the tech. "We need this in working order ASAP. Even if it's not a hundred percent. Understand?"

The tech looked up from the mess of gunk he was trying to scoop out of the inside of the weapon. "One shot. Don't care if it kills anyone in the local area?"

"It would be good if we didn't do the enemy's work for them, but yes."

"We need to let the others know what's going on," Whitnal said. "Even through the tree canopy, they'll know something happened. I'm surprised no one has come looking."

"It should be us. Me and Roger," the captain said. "Pen, join us. We'll be as quick as we can. We'll bring back help. Don't let anything happen to the prisoner. I won't start this colony on a vigilante killing."

Kalin was sure the words were meant for him and no one else. Of the people left at the clearing, only he might risk killing Brianne. "She'll be in one piece," he said. "We need to question her. And people need to witness justice happen."

"Let Weaver take care of her," the captain said. "Go to the command tent. Let the medics know what happened. See if you can gather any data from the ship. We don't need to be silent now. We need to be on alert and ready to react if we are given the opportunity."

React how? Kalin prayed that the end would come fast. Whether that was death, or life, they'd arrived at the end of a long journey. Tomorrow was the future, if they survived today.

Pen tugged at this arm. "Come on. We've got things to do."

He followed her and Jo from the shuttle, glancing up at the sky, the remaining ship had withdrawn so far it looked like a tiny moon.

Brianne, tied to the trunk of a tree across the clearing from the shuttle, her eyes on the ground, showed no sign of the defiance that drove her actions. She didn't look at them as they headed toward the command tent.

44

K alin knelt beside the two technicians who were wiping the last of the gunk from the workings.

"I don't like to leave it like this," the one tech said. "It's charging to the jury-rigged solar panel. One shot, but you choose between the strength of the contact or the distance."

"You should decide who'll be in here on ignition, too." The other tech stood and tossed his cleaning rags into a bin. "Let them say their goodbyes."

"You think the weapon will blow up?" Kalin asked.

Brianne had totally screwed them.

"We don't know," the first tech said. "It was only designed for one shot. It was built around one new Z-converter. Put in the used one? It could be fine, or lethal. We've done all we can."

"How long until the weapon is fully charged?" If it was going to cost a life, they should wait until the reward matched the risk.

"Give it an hour. But it still won't be a sure thing." The techs left him alone in the shuttle.

There was nothing for him to do inside but wait. He crossed the clearing again. Brianne remained attached to the tree, her guard in place. The walk to the command tent was long enough to give him time to come up with a strategy. Waiting was still an option, but people needed to move on. A day was almost gone since the enemy arrived. A day that felt like a year. The people in hiding would not stay there forever. The military would be itching to act, and soon Brianne wouldn't be the only one who dug them deeper by rash actions.

He arrived at the tent with only the vaguest recommendation in his mind, and glad he wasn't the one to make the final decision.

Inside he found five people: the captain, Whitnal, Pen, Jo, and Weaver. "The techs are done," he said.

The captain must have seen him scanning the tent. "We've been delegated the authority. The others are keeping the population quiet."

"Can we use the weapon?" Whitnal asked.

Kalin reported what the techs told him. "We need a volunteer if we attack."

"Brianne should be forced to do it," Pen said. "She put us in this position. She should risk her life."

"Do you think she will?" Weaver asked. "I mean, she just proved she can't be trusted."

"Do we really want to start our new life by killing her?" Whitnal asked. "She deserves to be punished, but ordering her to probable death is as bad as executing the woman."

"An hour before the weapon is ready," Kalin said. "That gives us time to call for a volunteer if we decide to finish off the remaining ship."

"Do we have a choice?" Weaver asked. "We don't need to

ask anyone outside to volunteer. I'm sure I'm not the only one here who will step up."

"That's not what I meant," Kalin said. "What about sending a scout to look for any activity around the ship? We can't let Brianne force our hand. Every question we had before she acted is still there."

"I'll go, captain," Jo said. "I'm the only one here who can fly a scout. I can send the coordinates."

Kalin looked at Pen. He hated that this would hurt her. Or if he was being honest, he hated that he would see her be hurt. But they needed intelligence. "I can fly a scout," he said. "Yours are similar to the ones I trained on."

Pen kept her eyes on the tabletop as she said, "We should send all three ships if they have enough fuel. It's not far, and three ships increase the odds that one makes it." Her voice was tight with emotion.

"Jo, fetch the other scouts," the captain said. "Pen is right, and they need to be part of the planning."

"The detection equipment is still aboard and functional," Whitnal said. "One could range out as far as possible and find out if other ships are on the way."

"Getting coordinates only works if the enemy doesn't move again." Weaver grabbed a ration bar and water, then headed for the door after Jo. "I'll make sure the prisoner is fed."

"He's right," Kalin said. "What are we hoping to learn when they approach?"

"Ranging out for other enemy ships approaching is a good idea," the captain said. "If the comms are working, the coordinates can be transmitted. If the scouts scatter, we can shoot."

"Maybe the techs were being pessimistic," Pen said.

"And maybe optimistic," Kalin said. "We should prepare for the worst."

The captain pulled papers into a pile. He checked the time and the door. "When the scouts get here, no more negative comments. You have a few minutes to make the case and then we are all onboard, right?"

Kalin nodded and saw Pen do the same.

"Here's what I think we are facing," the captain said. "An enemy with unknown capabilities and motives stands on our doorstep. We've just killed eighty percent of their ships. Our only weapon may or may not bring a decisive end to the situation. We have no intelligence to follow. We must protect the entirety of the human species."

"That sums it up," Pen said. "I hate it, but I don't see a way to end this peacefully. We can't let that ship simply sit in our sky. We won't survive under the threat."

"So, we send the scouts," Whitnal said. "We ask someone to sacrifice themselves to fire the weapon."

Tension drained from Kalin. Nothing had changed, but everything had changed. They were committing to do something. It didn't matter that the human race might be gone in a little over an hour. What mattered was they wouldn't be living with fear. Or not with physical evidence of life's fragility looming on the horizon every day.

"I'll tend to the weapon," he said. "I've been raised to sacrifice myself for the greater good. It's refreshing to volunteer rather than be ordered to do it."

Pen touched his shoulder. "I won't tell you not to do this. Just know I expect you to survive. Find a way to leave before any explosion."

He ignored everyone around them and hugged her into a kiss. "I am not ready to die," he said.

45

The weapon was charged as much as possible and sat ready to be used. Kalin waited for the orders to go to the shuttle, but so far, all that had happened was people rejoining them in the tent. And arguments over Brianne. It seemed she had a few friends still in the population. Perhaps she'd made promises of jobs in the colony, and they wanted her able to fulfill the promises. Kalin didn't give her future much thought.

Pen stuck with him. He'd tried to make her leave so he could settle his mind into the idea of dying, but she said she wasn't willing to lose any minutes with him. He stopped pushing her away after that.

"The comms are fixed," a tech called out. "Can't guarantee how long they will last."

The scouts ran to their ships. In five minutes, they would be punching through the atmosphere and trying to avoid being shot down while they gathered information.

"I should head out," Kalin said. "You can let me know when to fire."

"Not yet," the captain said. "There will be time for you to get to the clearing after the scouts report."

No one wanted to take the final steps until absolutely necessary. Kalin stayed near the door with Pen while he watched the action in the rest of the tent.

"Everyone knows this could be our last breaths on Damu." Pen leaned into him. "I wish you hadn't waited so long to tell me how you feel."

"Me too." *But maybe this would be harder if we had a chance to become closer.* "When this is over, we won't wait for anything."

"When this is over, I think we'll all want to sleep for a week," Pen said. "I know the gravity is a bit lighter than we had on the ship, but that won't keep us going forever; we will crash soon."

If we survive this, I won't be surprised if some rampaging herd of animals attacks us. Kalin kept the thought to himself. Any bit of optimism was precious right now.

"What's it like in the camp?" he asked.

"The last time I went the place looked more like a settlement than a camp. I claimed a tent for us, don't worry."

The comms came alive.

No action on the ship.

At my limit, no sign of reinforcements.

Shit, running out of fuel. On my way back.

Something is happening. Jo's voice cut off.

Kalin tensed, ready to sprint to the shuttle.

The captain nodded to the comms officer. "Need more, scout one."

Silence.

Then the sound of one scout returning, crashing through trees to land. No explosion, so Kalin dismissed the pilot from his thoughts.

I'm out too.

That left Jo alone at the ship. Why didn't he say something? Why didn't they get coordinates? Pen vibrated with tension in his arms.

They've launched what looks like a pod. Following.

If the enemy was coming to them, the weapon could sit idle.

"I'll meet the pod," Kalin said. "Alone."

"Get Jo's guess of a landing site," Pen said. "We'll both meet our visitor."

"No." Kalin stepped to the captain. "I go alone. If there's danger, I can deal with it."

It's going to land in the same clearing as the shuttle. Unless something changes.

"Jo will join you," the captain said and then turned to the comms operator. "Relay the order."

Pen followed him from the tent. "Wait. Why are you doing this?"

"I am the only one who can. No one will miss me in the settlement."

"I will."

"Thank you. But all this." He gestured to include the whole area, including the settlement. "This will still be successful. You will find someone else."

"How? If things go bad, you'll be gone. Jo will be gone. I might as well just be in the same danger too." Tears glistened in her eyes.

He pulled her close. "You are strong. I am not going to die today. I plan to come back with Jo. But who else is expendable? We need the guards to keep the peace. The leaders to guide the population. The medics and techs to keep people healthy. A civilian isn't ready to face whatever that pod holds."

She stepped out of his arms. "Fine. Just know that if you don't come back, I'm stuck hooking up with Asher."

He chuckled, glad she was smart enough to accept he was right. "At least wait until you're sure we're dead."

She pushed him toward the shuttle. "It probably makes sense for you to beat the pod to the clearing."

He waited for her return to the tent before sprinting toward the shuttle clearing.

Brianne still there at her tree, but her guard was untying the restraints.

"Better if she's not here to create more trouble," he said. "Glad the comms are up. Kind of missed knowing what was going on."

Then he was alone. He stood beside the shuttle, wishing he'd asked for an estimate of the pod's size. From here, the whole clearing was available. Jo's landing would probably be as hard as the other two scouts, if he even had the fuel to make it this far.

A rush of noise drew his attention to the trees behind him. Jo's ship slid into the clearing. He jumped out and joined Kalin as soon as it stopped.

"I got ahead of the pod," Jo said. "Maybe a couple of minutes until it gets here."

"How big?"

"It's round, but about the same volume as a small shuttle. Bigger than my ship anyway." Jo ran inside and returned with a water container. "You think they'll come out shooting?"

"Do you have a sidearm?" If he had to protect Jo as well as shoot an alien, Kalin needed to know now.

Jo pulled out a small stunner. "Let's hope they don't come close enough for me to use it."

Overhead, the sound of leaves shaking pulled his attention up. A large, round, white object dropped toward the clearing. Slowly, but on a course straight for the center.

"I guess all our questions are going to be answered in the next thirty seconds," Jo said. "What if they want to talk?"

"I guess we bring someone with the right skills." Kalin found it hard to imagine they would understand anything these aliens said. But the leaders of *The Righteous Storm* would not have given them the chance to try for peace.

46

Kalin stepped back, pulling Jo into the shelter of shuttle's open doorway. Being exposed when this thing landed seemed a stupid choice. Even if it was only a single pod, who knew what it carried. The enemy didn't need to blow up the planet in retaliation. In fact, they might not be able to avoid being caught in the corona of damage. A virus or a nerve agent would put an end to the colony without destroying a planet.

"Be ready to run," he said.

"Or not," Jo said. "It's not necessarily an attack."

"If it is, I'm hitting the ignition key on the weapon. If we have time for anything."

"Yeah, I'll be right behind you. If they are intent on destroying us, I want to hit back and stop them doing this to anyone else."

Kalin couldn't help thinking that if these aliens were intent on reaching out and making peace, they wouldn't have waited this long to do so.

The sound of wind through the trees became more violent, and then the pod touched down in the center of the clearing. A perfect ball of white. The coating didn't reflect anything, but Kalin thought he saw different shades of white swirling across the surface. A protective shield? An attempt to communicate?

The ball sat in the middle of the clearing as though waiting for them to do something.

"One of us should go out," Jo said. "If it attacks, the other hits the button."

"I'll go," Kalin said. "I came here for this, and I should be the one who takes the risk. You know how to fire this?" Kalin nodded back to the weapon.

"I know how to press a button. If something goes wrong, I'm lost. You?"

"I left that stuff to the techs."

"Should we report back?" Jo asked. "Comms are still live."

"You can do that." Kalin decided his sidearm should be in its holster. Not locked in, because if this pod didn't attack, he wanted to appear harmless but have a defense accessible. "I'm going."

Jo didn't make any effort to talk him out of acting, so Kalin stepped out of the shuttle and walked toward the pod. It hadn't landed, exactly. He could see a gap between the bottom of the white ball and the ground. When it left, if that's what was to happen, there would be no evidence of the vessel.

He walked a few steps farther and came to a stop. Time for the enemy to make a move.

It was hard to tell for sure, but Kalin had the sense that the pod was rotating. He couldn't imagine it would be possible to exit if that was so. Or not, maybe these beings didn't work the same way as humanoids.

A high-pitched whine crawled up Kalin's spine. Then

the sphere stopped spinning. The outer shell changed and started to reflect the clearing.

He'd been noticed.

"What do you want?" Kalin called out. Unlikely that they would speak English, but maybe they would recognize some kind of emotion, or just that he spoke.

The pod split vertically, and a small ball rolled out. The new object was about twenty-five centimeters in diameter. About the size of an environmental suit helmet. A representative? Kalin only saw black through the opening when the pod ejected it.

The whine crawled down his spine as the slit closed. Then the pod shot up into the sky, disappearing from sight in seconds.

"Let the captain know," Kalin called over to Jo.

"I did. He says to wait; they are on their way."

This might be a bomb.

"No. Tell them to stay back. I should check it out first."

Jo stepped beside him, comm in hand. "Yeah, that didn't work. The captain said to leave it alone until they arrive. He's bringing a team."

"Do you think we'll ever get rid of them?" Kalin nodded toward the enemy ship. "I almost want them to attack to end this weird waiting thing."

"Let us look at this," a tech said as she passed Kalin and Jo. "Is this the same material as the pod?"

Kalin confirmed it was and turned to the captain. "Sir, I don't think anyone else should touch this thing. The pod put it here when I called out. If there is a reason for that, we should find out."

The captain looked at the ball on the ground and then crouched beside it. "Look, the thing is floating."

"Pod did the same."

"I don't like asking, but try to lift it." He stepped back and called everyone to a safe distance.

Kalin considered the ball. If it sat on the ground, he'd have some idea how heavy it was. The thing could weigh less than a feather, or more than a planet. If the latter, there would surely be some effect on the feeling of gravity, and he didn't sense anything odd.

He reached out and placed his hand on the top of the ball, thinking to give a little pull before just picking it up. When his skin made contact, his hand tingled and stuck. The tingling increased to the point of pain. The device was taking samples. He pulled but his hand stuck there by some kind of field.

He heard Pen's voice, but she wasn't in the clearing. Then other voices murmured in his brain.

The colony.

As soon as he thought the words, the field let go. Kalin landed on his backside. Lights flickered across the surface of the ball and then went dead. The voices in his head vanished, and all he heard were the people in the clearing.

He stood and brushed the dirt from his butt as he looked up to see if the ship in orbit was making any moves to attack. The lights might have been the result of a report on the colonists. Information taken from his body.

The ship was getting smaller.

"It's leaving," the tech said.

Getting out of the blast range?

Kalin looked at the ball again. His spine reacted to the same kind of whine as before. A slit opened up and a small box popped out. The ball pixelated and fell to the ground, then disappeared into the soil.

"Kalin, step back," the captain said.

A tech scooped up a vial of the ground containing the

ball, placed a cordon around the area and said, "We'll analyze this. Check if there's any reason to worry, at least things we know about."

The box sat inside the cordon. Kalin started to say they should retrieve it when it flipped open to stand on the ground as a vertical black rectangle. A beam of light shone from the top. Then words. Kalin read them, and a gentle voice resonated in his brain at the same time.

"We are not interested in revenge. You may live in peace. We worry for the next creatures you encounter with your brutal actions."

47

K alin stepped out of the tent and into the morning sun. Pen was already at the fire, warming the leftovers of last night's feast. Damu's fauna and flora were all fit for human consumption. Kalin suspected the probe that found the planet so long ago had done something to ensure it became hospitable.

The first impression that the planet had been designed for humanity more than simply terraformed still fit. Their campground sloped gently toward a stream, the ground covered in close-growing blades like grass, but finer. The only danger they'd found so far was of getting a mild sunburn, and even that needed long exposure.

"Another good day," Pen said. "I know it's been a year, but I can't help feel that there has to be a bad weather season. Like there are multiple category-five storms building somewhere."

He was familiar with the feeling. Damu felt just a little too good to be true. "We've seen no evidence of storms, and the geologists have looked. Maybe the next generation will live without waiting for a disaster to happen."

Pen grunted her agreement and stirred the embers into a final boost of heat. "Tea?"

He accepted a cup and sat beside her. It worked better when she cooked. He did a much better job as dishwasher than chef. They planned on moving on today. This was the far end of the third exploration, and no signs of intelligent life had appeared. For them, or any of the five other teams out searching Damu.

"We'll be back in Damu One in a week," he said. "You want to visit Two? Have a vacation?"

The camp had split into two groups pretty quickly. The colonists in hiding weren't sitting in fear; they'd been planning and sorting out the settlement. After the enemy left, and the captain had shared the message, eventually people got over their anger at the accusation, and tired of the arguments about whether it was hypocrisy from the beings who'd annihilated a ship, or genuine from a separate race. The idea that they'd destroyed a potential ally had gained ground as time passed but ran out of steam since there was no way to confirm or refute it.

Then the explorers went out with specific goals. To find a place where farms and livestock could thrive. Damu One was administrative and artisans who produced clothes and tools, still too small to be called manufacturing centers. Two was farming. The livestock were still being cloned, but they would settle in Two.

The colony would grow as needed, but Kalin was glad for the option to explore with Pen. Jo worked with the leaders to plan the future out, and mostly, people just got on with life.

"It would be nice to see some of my friends in Two," Pen said. "Afterwards, I thought we should go looking for that water mass the scouts saw. Wouldn't it be nice to experience an ocean?"

The thought of that much open water didn't appeal, but neither did missing out on an adventure with Pen.

"You know, at some point in the future, no one will be looking for new places on Damu. I like us being the first humans to walk in places."

"At some point in the future, people will go back out to the stars." Pen handed him a plate of hash.

"An ocean sounds fun," Kalin said.

WANT MORE?

Use the QR code to find more science fiction books at pawilson.ca.

If you enjoyed reading ATTACK, please consider helping other readers to find the story by leaving a review.

FREE EBOOK

Claim your copy of Running the Game when you use the QR code below to sign up for my newsletter and cheer on Pen as she vies for a commission in the military.

ALSO BY PA WILSON

For more books by P A Wilson

Use the QR code below or go to pawilson.ca

ABOUT THE AUTHOR

Perry Wilson is a Canadian author based in Vancouver, BC who has big ideas and an itch to tell stories. Having spent some time on university, a career, and life in general, she returned to writing in 2008 and hasn't looked back since (well, maybe a little, but only while parallel parking).

She is a member of the Vancouver Writers Social Group, The Royal City Literary Arts Society, and The Surrey Writing Workshop. Perry has self-published several novels. She writes the Madeline Journeys, a fantasy series about a high-powered lawyer who finds herself trapped in a magical world, the Quinn Larson Quests, which follows the adventures of a wizard named Quinn who must contend with volatile fae in the heart of Vancouver, and the Charity Deacon Investigations, a mystery thriller series about a private eye who tends to fall into serious trouble with her cases, and The Riverton Romances, a series based in a small town in Oregon, one of her favorite states. Her stand-alone novels are Breaking the Bonds, Closing the Circle, and The Dragon at The Edge of The Map.

For more information
www.pawilson.ca
pawilson@pawilson.ca

ACKNOWLEDGMENTS

People think that the process of writing is solitary. That's not the case for me. I have help from so many people it would be hard to acknowledge everyone, but I'll give it a try.

The support and inspiration I get from my writer's groups is incalculable. The Vancouver Writers Social Group opens my mind to other ways of telling a story. The Royal City Literary Arts Society gives me the opportunity to meet and share with other writers who have more knowledge than I do. The Other 11 Months group is where I learn about getting the words on the page. And my critique group who helps me find the best parts of the story I want to tell. Thanks to all of the members of these great groups.

Last of all, but definitely a huge part of the process, my beta readers. These are the people who love stories and are willing, and more than able, to tell me if my finished story is ready for you, my readers.